Italian Royals

*Two royal medics—
can they find their perfect match?*

Take a trip through the cobbled streets of
Venice and discover the secrets that lie
within them in Annie O'Neil's decadent
duet! When a royal wedding is turned upside
down it sets in motion a truly unforgettable
and unexpected journey for Princess Beatrice
and her best friend and bridesmaid Fran.

Find out more in…

Tempted by the Bridesmaid

Bridesmaid Fran Martinelli's ideal
Italian summer goes south when she
turns up for work after the disaster
of her friend's wedding and finds out
the best man is her new boss!

Claiming His Pregnant Princess

When Princess Beatrice di Jesolo is jilted
by her royal fiancé she must hide her secret
pregnancy… A great idea until she discovers
her new boss is The One Who Got Away…

Available now!

Dear Reader,

Welcome to the first story of what I'm hoping you will think is a magical trip to Italy.

When I was dreaming up the perfect location for Luca, my tall, dark and dangerously handsome hero, I came across a website filled to the brim with photos of beautiful 'ghost towns' in Italy and simply had no choice but to get him to move into one.

This was an interesting book for me to write as it's the first time I've had a heroine who prefers working with dogs to people. After all, they're not only *man's* best friend, right? (*My* dogs are totally up there in the besties category.) And it took one very special human to bring Fran around to her HEA.

Enjoy—and don't be shy about getting in touch. You can reach me at annieoneilbooks.com, on Twitter @annieoneilbooks, or find me on Facebook...

Annie O' xx

TEMPTED
BY THE
BRIDESMAID

BY
ANNIE O'NEIL

Published in Great Britain 2017
By Mills & Boon, an imprint of HarperCollins*Publishers*
1 London Bridge Street, London, SE1 9GF

© 2017 Annie O'Neil

ISBN: 978-0-263-06955-6

Our policy is to use papers that are natural, renewable and recyclable
products and made from wood grown in sustainable forests. The logging
and manufacturing processes conform to the legal environmental
regulations of the country of origin.

Printed and bound in Great Britain
by CPI Antony Rowe, Chippenham, Wiltshire

Annie O'Neil spent most of her childhood with her leg draped over the family rocking chair and a book in her hand. Novels, baking, and writing too much teenage angst poetry ate up most of her youth. Now Annie splits her time between corralling her husband into helping her with their cows, baking, reading, barrel racing (not really!) and spending some very happy hours at her computer, writing.

Books by Annie O'Neil

Mills & Boon Medical Romance

Paddington Children's Hospital
Healing the Sheikh's Heart

Hot Latin Docs
Santiago's Convenient Fiancée

Christmas Eve Magic
The Nightshift Before Christmas

The Monticello Baby Miracles
One Night, Twin Consequences

One Night...with Her Boss
London's Most Eligible Doctor
Her Hot Highland Doc

Visit the Author Profile page
at millsandboon.co.uk for more titles.

This book could go to no other than Jorja and Grissom—
my own fluffy hounds, who are always there
when I need them…and sometimes when I don't!

Furry friends…simply the best!

CHAPTER ONE

IT FELT AS if she were watching the world through a fish-bowl. Everything was distorted. Sight. Sound. Fran would have paid a million dollars to be anywhere else right now.

Church silence was crushing. Especially under the circumstances.

Fran looked across to the groomsmen. Surely there was an ally within that pack of immaculately suited Italian gentry who...?

Hmm... Not you, not you, not you... Oh!

Fran caught eyes with one of them. Gorgeous, like the rest, but his brow was definitely more furrowed, the espresso-rich eyes a bit more demanding than the others... Oh! Was that a scar? She hadn't noticed last night at the candlelit cocktail party. *Interesting.* She wondered what it would feel like to—

"Ahem!" The priest—or was he a bishop?—cleared his throat pointedly.

Why had she raised her hand? This wasn't school—it was a church!

This wasn't even Fran's wedding, and yet the hundreds of pairs of eyes belonging to each and every esteemed guest sitting in Venice's ridiculously beautiful basilica were trained on *her*. Little ol' Francesca "Fran" Martinelli, formerly of Queens, New York, now of...well...

nowhere, really. It was just her, the dogs, a duffel bag
stuffed to the hilt with more dog toys than clothes and
the very, *very* pretty bridesmaid's dress she was wearing.

Putting it on, she'd actually felt girlie! Feminine. It
would be back to her usual jeans and T-shirt tomorrow,
though, when she showed up for her new mystery job.
In the meantime, she was failing at how to be a perfect
bridesmaid on an epic scale.

Fran's fingers plucked at the diaphanous fabric of her
azure dress and she finally braved looking straight into
the dark brown eyes of her dearest childhood friend,
Princess Beatrice Vittoria di Jesolo.

The crowning glory of their shared teenage years had
been flunking out of finishing school together in Switzerland. That sun-soaked afternoon playing hooky had
been an absolute blast. Sure, they'd been caught, but did
anyone really *care* if you could walk with a book on
your head?

Their friendship had survived the headmistress dress-
ing them down in front of their more civilized classmates,
grass stains on their jeans, scrapes on their hands and
knees from scrabbling around in the mountains making
daisy chains and laughing until tears shot straight out of
their eyes... But this moment—the one where Fran was
ruining her best friend's wedding in front of the whole
universe—this might very well spell the end of their
friendship. The one thing she could rely on in her life.

Fran squeezed her eyes tight against Bea's inquiring
gaze. The entire veil-covered, bouquet-holding, finger-
waiting-for-a-ring-on-it image was branded onto her
memory bank. Never mind the fact that there were of-
ficial photographers lurking behind every marble pillar,
and hundreds of guests—including dozens of members of
Europe's royal families—filling the pews to overflowing,

not to mention the countless media representatives waiting outside to film the happy power couple once they had been pronounced husband and wife.

Which they would be doing in about ten minutes or so unless she got her act together and did something!

"What exactly is your objection?" asked the man with the mystery scar through gritted teeth. In English. Which was nice.

Not because Fran's Italian was rusty—it was all she and her father ever spoke at home…when she *was* at home—but because it meant not every single person in the church would know that she'd just caught Bea's fiancé playing tonsil tennis with someone who wasn't Bea.

She stared into the man's dark eyes. Did *he* know? Did he care that the man he was standing up for in front of Italy's prime guest list was a lying cheat?

"If you could just speak up, dear," the priest tacked on, a bit more gently.

Maybe the priest didn't want to know specifically what her objection was—was choosing instead just to get the general gist that everything wasn't on the up-and-up. That or he would clap his hands, smile and say "Surprise! I saw them, too. The wedding's off because the groom's a cheat. He's just been having it off with the maid of dishonor in the passage to the doge's palace. So…who's ready for lunch?"

After another quick eye-scrunch, Fran eased one eye open and scanned the scene.

Nope. Beatrice was still standing next to her future husband, just about to be married. All doe-eyed and… well…maybe not totally doe-eyed. Beatrice had always been the pragmatic one. But—*oh, Dio! C'è una volpe sciolto nel pollaio*, as her father said whenever things were completely off-kilter. Which they were. Right now.

Right here. A fox was loose in the hen house of Venice's most holy building, where a certain groom should have been hit by a lightning bolt or something by now.

On the plus side, Fran had the perfect position to give the groom the evil eye. Marco Rodolfo. Heir apparent to some royal title or other, here in the Most Serene Republic of Venice, and recent ascendant to the throne of a ridiculously huge fortune.

Money wasn't everything. She knew that from bitter experience. Truth was a far more valuable commodity. At least she hoped that was what Bea would think when she finally managed to open her mouth and speak.

Maybe she could laser beam a confession out of him…

The groom looked across at Fran…caught her gaze… and smiled. In its smarmy wake she could have sworn that a glint, a zap of light striking a sharp blade, shot across at her.

Go on, the smile said. *I dare you.*

Marco "The Wolf" Rodolfo.

The wolf indeed. He hadn't even bothered with the sheep's clothing. If she looked closely, would she see extra-long incisors? *All the better to eat you—*

"*Per favore, signorina?*"

A swirl of perfectly coiffured heads whipped her way as the priest gave her an imploring look. Or was he a cardinal? She really should have polished up her knowledge of the finer details of her Catholic childhood. Church, family dinners, tradition… They'd all slipped away when her mother had left for husband number two and her father had disappeared with a swan dive into his work.

"Francesca!" Bea growled through a fixed smile. "Any clues?"

Santo cielo! This was exactly the reason her father had held her at arm's length all these years. She couldn't keep her mouth shut, could she? Always had to speak the truth, no matter what the consequences.

"Francesca?"

"He's—" Fran's index finger took on a life of its own and she watched as it started lifting from her side to point at the reason why Bea's wedding shouldn't go ahead. She couldn't even look at the maid of honor he'd been having his wicked way with. What was her name? Marina? Something like that. The exact sort of woman who always made her feel more tomboy than Tinker Bell. Ebony tresses to her derriere. Willowy figure. Cheekbones and full lips that gave her an aloof look. Or maybe she looked that way because she actually *was* aloof.

She was insincere and a fiancé thief—that much was certain. Since when did Bea hang out with such supermodelesque women anyhow?

Society weddings.

Total. Nightmare.

Last night, in their two seconds alone, Bea had muttered something about out-of-control guest lists, her mother and bloodline obligations. All this while staring longingly at Fran's glass of champagne and then abruptly calling it a night. Not exactly the picture of a bride on the brink of a lifetime of bliss. A bride on the brink of disaster, more like.

"Francesca, say something!"

All Fran could do was stare wide-eyed at her friend. Her beautiful, kind, honest, wouldn't-hurt-a-fly, take-no-prisoners friend. This was life being mean. Cruel, actually. When she'd seen Mommy kissing someone who definitely hadn't been Santa Claus and told her father about it, how had she been meant to know that her mother would leave her father and break his heart?

Would Bea stay friends with the messenger now, or

hate her forever? A bit like Fran's father had hated her since his marriage blew apart no matter how hard she'd tried to gain his approval. A tiny hit of warmth tickled around her heart. They were going to try again. *Soon.* He'd promised.

The tickle turned ice-cold at another throat-clearing prompt from Mr. Sexy.

Why, why, why was *she* the one who caught all the cheaters in the world?

All the eyes on her felt like laser beams.

Including the eyes of the mystery groomsman who she really *would* have liked to get to know a bit better if things had been different. *Typical.* Timing was definitely not her forte. What was his name? Something sensual. Definitely not Ugolino, as her aunt had mysteriously called her son. No…it was something more…*toothsome.* A name that tantalized your tongue, like amaretto or a perfectly textured gelato. Cool and warming all at once. Something like the ancient city of…

Luca! That was his name.

Luca. He was filling out his made-to-measure suit with the lean, assured presence of a man who knew his mind. His crisp white shirt collar highlighted the warm olive tone of his skin and the five-o'clock shadow that was already hinting at making an appearance, despite the fact it was still morning. He looked like a man who would call a spade a spade.

Which might explain why he was staring daggers at her. Strangely, the glaring didn't detract from his left-of-center good looks. He wasn't one of those calendar-ready men whose perfection was more off-putting than alluring. Sure, he had the cheekbones, the inky dark hair and brown eyes that held the mysteries of the universe in them, but he also had that scar. A jagged one that looked as if it could tell a story or two. It dissected his left eyebrow, skipped the eye, then shot along his cheek. If she wasn't wrong, there were a few tiny ones along his chin, too. Little faint scars she might almost have reached out and touched—if his lips hadn't been moving.

"*Per amor del cielo!* Put these poor people out of their misery!"

Fran blinked. Enigmatic-scar man was right.

She looked to his left. The priest-bishop-cardinal was speaking to her again. Asking her to clarify why she believed this happy couple should not lawfully be joined in marriage. Murmurs of dismay were audibly rippling through the church behind her. Part of her was certain she could hear howls from the paparazzi as they waited outside to pounce.

Clammy prickles of panic threatened to consume her brain.

Friends didn't let friends marry philandering liars. Right? Then again, what did *she* know? She was Italian by birth, but raised in America. Maybe a little last-minute nookie right before you married your long-term intended was the done thing in these social circles filled with family names that went back a dozen generations or more. It wasn't illegal, but... Oh, this was ranking up there in worst-moments-ever territory!

Fran sucked in a deep breath. It was the do-or-die moment. Her heart was careening around her chest so haphazardly she wouldn't have been surprised if it had flown straight out of her throat, but instead out came words. And before she could stop herself, she heard herself saying to Beatrice, "He's... You can't marry him!"

CHAPTER TWO

"Basta!" Quick as a flash, Luca shuttled the key players in this farce to the back of the altar, then down a narrow marble passageway until they reached an open but mercifully private corridor.

"Her dress was up and Marco—"

"Per favore. I implore you to just…*stop.*" Luca whirled around, only to receive a full-body blow from the blonde bridesmaid. As quickly as the raft of sensations from holding her in his arms hit him she pressed away from him—*hard.*

"I'm just trying—" Bea's friend clamped her full, pink lips tight when her eyes met his.

The rest of the party was moving down the corridor as Luca wrestled with her revelation. "Do you have *any* idea what you've done? The damage you've caused?"

Stillness enveloped her as his words seemed to take hold.

Such was the power of the moment, Luca was hurtled back to a time and place when he, too, had been incapable of motion. Only there had been a doctor *and* a priest then.

Stillness had been the only way to let the news sink in.

Mother. Father. His sister, her husband—all of them save his beautiful niece. Gone. And *he'd* been the one behind the wheel.

He closed his eyes and willed the memory away, forcing himself to focus on the bridesmaid in front of him. Still utterly stationary—a deer in the headlights.

Another time, another place he would have said she was pretty. Beautiful, even. Honey-gold hair. Full, almost-pouty lips he didn't think had more than a slick of gloss on them. Eyes so blue he would have sworn they were a perfect match to the Adriatic Sea not a handful of meters from the basilica.

"Don't you dare—" She took in a jagged breath, tears filming her eyes. "Don't you *dare* tell me I don't understand what speaking up means."

Luca's gut tightened as she spoke. Behind those tears there was nothing but honesty. The type of honesty that would change everything.

His mind reeled through the facts. Beatrice was one of his most respected friends. They'd known each other all their lives and had been even closer during med school. Their career trajectories had shot them off in opposite directions, much to their parents' chagrin. He'd not missed their hints, their hopes that their friendship would blossom into something more.

Beautiful as Beatrice was, theirs would always be a platonic relationship. When she'd taken up with Marco he'd almost been relieved. *Si*, he had a playboy's reputation, but he was a grown man now. A prince with an aristocratic duty to fulfill—a legacy to uphold. When Marco had asked him to be best man he'd been honored. Proud, even, to play a role in Beatrice's wedding.

Cheating just minutes before he was due to marry? What kind of man would *do* that?

He shot a glance at Marco, who was raising his hands in protest before launching into an impassioned appeal to both Bea and the cardinal.

Marco and a bridesmaid in a premarital clinch? As much as he hated to admit it, he couldn't imagine it was the type of thing a true friend would conjure up just to add some drama to Italy's most talked-about wedding.

He glanced down at her hands, each clutching a fistful of the fairy-tale fabric billowing out from her dress in the light wind. No rings.

A Cinderella story, perhaps? The not-so-ugly stepsister throwing a spanner into the works, hoping to catch the eye of the Prince?

Each time she pulled at her dress she revealed the fact that she was actually wearing flip-flops in lieu of any Italian woman's obligatory heels. No glass slippers, then. Just rainbow-painted toes that would have brought the twitch of a smile to his lips if his mind hadn't been racing for ways to fend off disaster.

She'd be far less high maintenance than his only-the-best-will-do girlfriend.

He shook off this reminder that he and Marina needed "a talk" and forced himself to meet the blonde's gaze again. Tearstained but defiant. A surge of compassion shot through him. If what she was saying was true she was a messenger who wouldn't escape unscathed.

"I saw them!" she insisted, tendrils of blond hair coming loose from the intricate hairdo the half-dozen or so bridesmaids were all wearing. All of the bridesmaids including *his* girlfriend. "It's not like you're the one who's been cheated on," she whisper-hissed, her blue eyes flicking toward Beatrice, who, unlike her, was remaining stoically tear-free.

Luca took hold of her elbow and steered her farther away from the small group, doing his best to ignore how soft her skin felt under the work-hardened pads of his fingertips. Quite a change from the soft-as-a-surgeon's hands he'd been so proud of. Funny what a bit of un-expected tragedy could do to a man.

"Perhaps we should leave the bride and groom to chat with the cardinal." A shard of discord lodged in his spine as he heard himself speak. It had been in the icy tone he'd only ever heard come out of his mouth once before. The day his father had confessed he'd gambled away the last of the family's savings.

"I'm Francesca, by the way," she said, as if adding a personal touch would blunt the edges of this unbelievable scenario. Or perhaps she was grasping at straws, just as he was. "I think I saw you at the cocktail party last night."

"I would say it's a pleasure to meet you, but…"

She waved away his platitudes. They both knew they were beyond social niceties.

"Francesca…" He drew her name out on the premise of buying time. He caught himself tasting it upon his tongue as one might bite into a lemon on a dare, surprised to find it sweet when he had been expecting the bitterness of pith, the sourness of an unripe fruit.

Focus, man.

Luca clenched his jaw so tightly he saw Francesca's eyes flick to the telltale twitch in his cheek. The one with the scar.

Let her stare.

He swallowed down the hit of bile that came with the thought. He knew better than most that nothing good came from a life built on illusion.

"I don't think I need to remind you what our roles are here. I promised to be best man at this wedding. To vouch for the man about to marry our mutual friend."

He moved closer toward her and caught a gentle waft of something. Honeysuckle with a hint of grass? His eyes met hers and for a moment…one solitary moment…they were connected. Magnetically. Sensually.

Luca stepped back and gave his jaw a rough scrub, far too aware that Francesca had felt it, too.

"There is no one in the world I would defend more than Bea." Francesca's words shattered the moment, forcing him to confront reality. "And, believe me, of all the people standing here I *know* how awful this is."

Something in her eyes told him she wasn't lying. Something in his heart told him he already knew the truth.

"I'd want to know," she insisted. "Wouldn't you?"

Luca looked away from the clear blue appeal in her eyes, redirecting the daggers he was shooting toward her to the elaborately painted ceiling of the marble-and-flagstone passageway. The hundreds of years it had taken to build the basilica evaporated to nothing in comparison to the milliseconds it had taken to grind this wedding to a halt.

A wedding. A marriage. It was meant to last a lifetime.

"Of course I'd want to know," he bit out. "But your claims are too far-fetched. The place where you're saying you saw them is not even private."

"I know! It doesn't mean it didn't happen."

Francesca's eyes widened and the tears resting on her eyelids cascaded onto her cheeks before zipping down to her chin and plopping unceremoniously into the hollow of her throat. Luca only just stopped himself from lifting both his hands to her collarbone and swiping them away with his thumbs. First one, then the other… Perhaps tracing the path of one of those tears slipping straight between the soft swell and lift of—

Focus!

"Which one was it? Which woman?"

Francesca's blue eyes, darkened with emotion, flicked up and to the right. "She had dark hair. Black."

The information began to register in slow motion. Not Suzette…a flame-bright redhead. And the others were barely into their teens.

Elimination left him with only one option.

A fleeting conversation with his girlfriend came back to him. One in which he'd said he was going to be too busy with the clinic to come to the wedding. Marina had been fine with it. Had agreed, in fact. *So* much work at the clinic, she'd said. And then it all fell into place. The little white lies. The deceptions. The ever-increasing radio silences he hadn't really noticed in advance of the clinic's opening day.

A coldness took hold of his entire chest. An internal ice storm wrought its damage as the news fully penetrated.

"My girlfriend was *not* having sex with Marco."

Francesca's eyes pinged wide, a hit of shock shuddering down her spine before she managed to respond.

"Your girlfriend? That's… *Wow.*" She shook her head in disbelief. "For the record, she is an idiot. If you were *my* boyfriend, lock and key might be more—"

Luca held up a hand. He didn't want to hear it.

It was difficult to know whether to be self-righteous or furious. In Rome, his relationships had hardly warranted the title. Since moving back to Mont di Mare…

The home truths hit hard and fast. Sure, Marina had been complaining that she wasn't the center of his universe lately, but any fool—anyone with a heart beating in their chest—could have seen that his priorities were not wooing and winning right now.

He owed every spare ounce of his energy to his niece.

The one person who'd suffered the most in that horrific car accident. His beautiful, headstrong niece, confined to a wheelchair evermore.

He looked across at Marco. The sting of betrayal hit hard and fast.

He and Marina had never been written in the stars—but *Beatrice*? A true princess if ever there was one. She was shaking her head. Holding up a hand so that Marco would stop his heated entreaty. From where Luca was standing it didn't look as if the wedding would go ahead.

He swore under his breath. He had trusted Marco to treat Bea well—cautioned him about his rakish past and then congratulated him with every fiber of his being when at long last he'd announced his engagement to Princess Beatrice Vittoria di Jesolo.

The three of them had shared the same upbringing. Privileged. Exclusive. Full of expectation—no, more than that, full of *obligation* that they would follow in their ancestors' footsteps. Marry well. Breed more titled babies.

Luca might have considered the same future for himself before the accident. But that had all changed now. Little wonder Marina had strayed. He'd kept her at arm's length. Farther away. It was surprising she had stayed any time at all.

"Why don't you go and get her? Ask her yourself?" Francesca wasn't even bothering to swipe at the tears streaking her mascara across her cheeks.

"You're absolutely positive?"

Even as the hollow-sounding words left his mouth he knew they were true. There weren't that many women wandering around the basilica in swirls of weightless ocean-blue fabric. And there was only one bridesmaid with raven hair. The same immaculate silky hair he'd been forbidden from touching that morning when Marina had popped into the hotel suite to grab the diamante clutch bag she'd left while she was at the hairdresser's. Not so immaculate when she'd appeared at the altar, looking rosy cheeked and more alive than he'd seen her in months, if he was being honest.

"I—I can go get her for you, if you like," Francesca offered after hiccuping a few more tears away.

He had to hand it to her. The poor woman was crying her eyes out, but she knew how to stand her ground.

"Why don't I go find her?" Her fingers started doing a little nervous dance in the direction of the church, where everyone was still waiting.

"No offense, but you are the *last* person I would ever ask to help me."

"Isn't it better to know the truth than to live a lie?"

Luca swore softly and turned away. She was hitting just about every button he didn't care to admit he had. Truth. Deceit. Honesty. Lies. Weakness.

He had no time in his life for weakness. No capacity for lies.

He forced himself to look Francesca in the eye, knowing there wasn't an iota of kindness in his gaze. But he still couldn't give in to the innate need to feel empathy for the position she'd been put in. Or compassion for the tears rising again and again, glossing her eyes and then falling in a steady trickle along her tear-soaked face. How easy it would be to lift a finger and just...

Magari!

Shooting the messenger was a fool's errand, but he didn't know how else to react... A knife of rage swept through him. If he never thought about Marina or Marco again it would be too soon.

"It didn't seem like it was the first time," Francesca continued, her husky voice starting to break in a vain attempt to salve the ever-deepening wound. "I'm happy to go and get her if you want."

"Basta! Per favore!"

No need to paint a picture. He almost envied Francesca. Seeing in an instant what he should have known for weeks. He should have ended it before she'd even thought to stray.

"If you want, I'll do it. Go and get her. I would do it for any friend."

Francesca shifted from one foot to the other, eyes glued to his, waiting for his response. He'd be grateful for this one day, but right now Francesca was the devil's messenger and he'd heard enough.

The words came to him—jagged icicles shooting straight from his arctic heart. "I know you mean well, Francesca, but you and I will *never* be friends."

Shell-shocked. That was how Bea had looked for the rest of the day. Not that Fran could blame her. Talk about living a nightmare. She knew better than most that coming to terms with deception on that kind of scale could take years. A lifetime, even, if her father's damaged heart was anything to go by.

From the look on Luca's face when they'd finally parted at the basilica he was going to need *two* lifetimes to get over his girlfriend's betrayal. Good thing they wouldn't be crossing paths anytime soon.

"Want me to see if I can find a case of prosecco lying around? A karaoke machine? We could sing it out and down some fizz."

Fran scanned the hotel suite. The caterers had long been sent away, the decorations had been removed and the staff instructed to keep any and all lurking paparazzi as far away as possible…

"No, thanks, *cara*. Maybe some water?" Bea asked.

"On it."

As she poured a glass of her friend's favorite—sparkling water from the alpine region of Italy—Fran was even more in awe of her friend's strength. All tucked up in bed, makeup removed, dress unceremoniously wilting like a deflated meringue in the bathroom, Bea looked exhausted, but not defeated.

"Want to tell me anything about this mystery job I'm due to start tomorrow?"

"No." Bea took a big gulp of water and grinned, obviously grateful for the change of topic. "Although it *will* make use of both your physio skills and the assistance dogs."

Fran frowned. "I thought you said she had a doctor looking after her?"

Bea blinked, but said nothing.

"The girl's in a wheelchair, right? Lower extremities paralyzed?"

"Yeah, but…" Bea tipped her head to the side and gave her friend a hard look. "You're not going to waste all those years of practicing physio are you?"

"What? Because the person I was stupid enough to go into business with saw me as a limitless supply of cash?"

"You're clear of that, though, aren't you?"

Fran grunted.

People? Disappointing. Dogs? They never asked for a thing. Except maybe a good scratch around the ears.

"Are you sure you're all right?" Fran flipped the topic back to Bea. "Don't you want to stay in the palazzo with your family?"

"And listen to my mother screech on about the disaster of the century? How I've ruined the family's name. The family's genetic line. Any chance of happiness for

the di Jesolos forever and ever. Not a chance. Besides—"
she scanned the sumptuous surroundings of the room
"—your suite is great and I'd much rather be with you,
even if the place *does* smell all doggy."

"Does not." Fran swiped at the air between them with
a grin. She'd washed the dogs to within an inch of their
lives before they'd checked into Venice's fanciest hotel.
A little trust-fund treat to herself before heading out to
this mystery village where Bea had organized her summer job.

"You don't need to watch over me, you know," Bea
chided gently. "I'm not going to do anything drastic. And
you *are* allowed to take the dress off. Don't know if
you've heard, but the wedding's off!"

"Just wanted to get my money's worth!" Fran said,
knowing the quip was as lame as it sounded.

The truth was, she hadn't felt so pretty in...*years*, really. When your workaholic dad bought your clothes from
the local menswear shop, there was only so much ironic
style a girl could pull off. When she'd graduated to buying her own clothes it had felt like a betrayal even to
glance at something pink and frilly. It wasn't *practical*.

*"Not exactly what a proper engineer would wear,
Frannie!"*

So much for *that* pipe dream! It had died along with
a thousand others before she'd found her niche in the
world of physiotherapy and then, even more perfectly, in
assistance-dog training. *Dogs.* They were who she liked
to spend her time with. They were unconditionally loyal
and always ridiculously happy to see her. When she had
to hand over these two dogs to her mystery charge at the
end of the summer...

Fran swallowed down another rush of tears. Bea
shouldn't have to be the one being stoic here. "I'm so

sorry, Bea. About doing things the way I did. There just wasn't time to catch you after I'd seen them, and before I knew it, we were all up there at the altar and—"

"I'm not sorry at all." Bea said. "I'm glad you said something. Grateful you had the courage when no one else did."

"That's pretty magnanimous for someone who just found out they were being cheated on!"

"Others knew. All along. Even my mother." Bea chased up the comment with a little typical eye roll.

Fran's hands flew to cover her mouth. *Wow.* That was just… *Wow.*

"They were all so desperate for me to be one half of the most enviable couple in Europe. Even if it came at a cost." She shuddered away the thought. "You were the only one today who was a true friend."

Fran's tear ducts couldn't hold back any longer.

"How can you be so nice about everything when I've ruined the best day of your life?"

"*Amore!* Stop. You were *not* the one who ruined the day. Besides, I'm pretty sure there will be another best day of my life," Bea added, with a hint of something left unsaid in her voice.

"Since I barely see you once a year, it would've been nice to be honest about something else. Like how ridiculously beautiful you looked today."

Fran's heart rose into her throat as at long last Bea's eyes finally clouded with tears.

"Everyone has their secrets," Bea whispered.

"Including you?"

Bea looked away. Fair enough. There had to be a full-blown tropical storm going on in that head of hers right now, and if she wanted to keep her thoughts to herself, she was most deserving. Thank heavens her family had the financial comfort to sort out the mess The Wolf's infidelity would leave in its wake.

"You all ready for your new job?" Bea turned back toward her with a soft smile.

"Yes!" She gave an excited clap of her hands. The two dogs she had trained up for this job were amazing. "Not that you've told me much about the new boss, apart from the pro bono bit. I can't *believe* you offered to pay me."

Beatrice scrunched her features together. "Best not to mention that."

"I have no problem doing it for free. You know that. If I could've lived in one place for more than five minutes over the past few years, I would've set up a charitable trust through Martinelli Motors years ago, but…"

"*He* was too busy making his mark?"

"As ever. We don't have ancient family lineage to rely on like you do."

"*Ugh.* Don't remind me."

"Sorry…" Fran cringed, then held her arms open wide to the heavens. "Please help me stop sticking my foot in my mouth today!" She dropped her arms and pulled her friend into a hug. "Ever wished you'd just stayed in England?"

Bea's eyes clouded and again she looked away. This time Fran had *definitely* said the wrong thing, brought up memories best left undisturbed.

"That was…" Bea began, stopping to take a faltering breath. "That was a very special time and place. Those kinds of moments only come once in a lifetime."

Fran pulled back from the hug and looked at her friend, lips pressed tight together. She wouldn't mention Jamie's name if Beatrice didn't. The poor girl had been through enough today without rehashing romances of years gone by.

"Right!" Fran put on a jaunty grin. "Time to totally change the topic! Now, as my best friend, won't you please give me just a teensy, tiny hint about my new boss so I don't ruin things in the first five minutes?"

"*You're* the one who wanted a mystery assignment!"

"I didn't want them to know who *I* was—not the other way around!" Fran shot Bea a playful glower.

She'd already been burned by a business partner who had known she was heiress to her father's electric-car empire. And when it came to her social life, people invariably got the wrong idea. Expected something...*someone*...more glamorous, witty, attention seeking, party mad.

It was why she'd given up physio altogether. Dogs didn't give a damn about who she was so long as she was kind and gave them dinner. If only her new boss was a pooch! She giggled at the thought of a dog in a three-piece suit and a monocle.

"What's so funny?" Bea asked.

"C'mon...just give me a little new-boss hint," Fran cajoled, pinching her fingers together so barely a sheet of paper could pass between them.

Bea shook her head no. "I've told you all you need to know. The girl's a teenager. She's been in a wheelchair for a couple of years now. Paraplegic after a bad car accident. Very bad. Her uncle—"

"Ooh! There's an enigmatic *uncle*?"

"Something like that," Bea intoned, wagging her finger. "No hints. They need the dog so she can be more independent."

"*She* needs the dog."

"Right. That's what I said."

"You said *they* need the dog," Fran wheedled, hoping

to get a bit more information, but Bea just made an invisible zip across her lips. *No more.*

"That's not tons to go on, you know. I've been forced to bring two dogs to make sure I've got the right one!"

"Forced?" Bea cackled. "Since when have you had to be *forced* to travel with more than one dog?"

"C'mon…" Fran put her hands into a prayer position. "Just tell me what her parents are like—"

Beatrice held up her hand. "No parents. They both died in the same accident."

"Ouch." Fran winced. She'd lost her mother to divorce and her father to work. Losing them for real must be devastating.

"So does that mean this devilishly handsome uncle plays a big role in her life?"

"No one said he was handsome!" Bea admonished. "And remember—good things come to those who wait!"

Bea took on a mysterious air and, if Fran wasn't mistaken, there was also an elusive something else she couldn't quite put her finger on. How could a person *glow* when their whole life had just been ripped out from beneath them? Bea was in a league of her own. There weren't too many people who would set up a dream job for a friend who was known to dip in and out of her life like a yo-yo.

"Well, even if her uncle is a big, hairy-eared ogre, I can't wait. Nothing beats matching the right pooch to the right patient." Fran couldn't stop herself from clapping a bit more, drawing the attention of her two stalwart companions. "C'mere, pups! Help me tuck in Her Majesty."

Bea batted at the air between them. "No more royal speak! I don't want to be reminded."

"What?" Fran fell into their lifelong patter. "The fact that you're so royal you'd probably bleed fleurs-de-lys?"

"That's the French, idiot!"

"What do Italian royals bleed, then? Truffles?"

"Ha!" Bea giggled, reaching out a hand to give Fran's a big squeeze. "It's not truffle season. It's tabloid season. And they're *definitely* going to have a field day with this. I can't even bear to think about it." She threw her arm across her eyes and sank back into the downy pillow. "What do you think they'll say? Princess left at the altar, now weeping truffle tears?"

Fran pulled her friend up by her hands and gave her a hug. It was awful seeing her beautiful dark eyes cloud over with sadness. "How about some honey?" she suggested, signaling to the two big dogs to come over to the bedside. "That mountain honey you gave me from the Dolomites was amazing."

"From the resort?" Bea's eyes lit up at the thought. "It's one of the most beautiful places in the world. Maybe…"

"Maybe what?" Fran knew the tendrils of a new idea when she saw one.

"Maybe I'll pull a Frannie!"

"What does *that* mean?" She put on an expression of mock horror, fully aware that it wasn't masking her defensive reaction.

She knew exactly what it meant. A lifetime of trying to get her father's attention and failing had turned her into a wanderer. Staying too long in any one place meant getting attached. And that meant getting hurt.

"Don't get upset. I envy you. Your ability to just pick up and go. Disappear. Reinvent yourself. Maybe it's time *I* went and did something new."

Fran goldfished for a minute.

"That phase of my life might be over," she hedged. "Once this summer's done and dusted I'm going home."

"*Home*, home?" Bea sat up straight, eyes wide with shock. "I thought you said you'd never settle down there."

"Dad's offered to help me set up a full-time assistance-dogs training center—"

"You've never accepted his money before! What's the catch?"

"You mean what's going to be different this time?" Fran said, surprised at the note of shyness in her voice.

Bea nodded. She was the one who had always been there on the end of a phone when Fran had called in tears. *Again.*

"We spent a week together before I came over."

"A *week*?" Bea's eyes widened in surprise. "That's huge for you two. He wasn't in the office the whole time?"

"Nope! We actually went to a car show together."

Bea pursed her lips together. Not impressed.

"I know. I know," Fran protested, before admitting, "He had a little run-in with the pearly gates."

"Fran! Why didn't you *tell* me?"

"It turned out to be one of those cases of indigestion disguising itself as a heart attack, but it seems to have been a lightbulb moment for him. Made him reassess how he does things."

"You mean how he's neglected his only daughter most of his life?"

"It wasn't *that* bad."

"Francesca Martinelli, don't you *dare* tell me your heart wasn't broken time and time again by your father choosing work over spending time with you."

Fran met her friend's gaze—saw the unflinching truth in it, the same solid friendship and loyalty she'd shown her from the day they'd met at boarding school.

"I know. But this time it really *is* different."

"Frannie..." Bea's brow furrowed. "He took you to a *car* show. You *hate* cars!"

"It was an antique car show. Not a single electric car in sight."

Bea gave a low whistle. "Will wonders never cease?"

"Martinelli Motors is doing so well it could probably run itself."

"No surprise there. But I'm still amazed he took time off. It must've been one heck of a health scare."

Fran nodded. She knew Bea's wariness was legitimate. The number of times Fran had thought *this* would be the time her father finally made good on his promise to spend some quality father-daughter time...

"It was actually quite sweet. I got to learn a lot more about him as we journeyed through time via the cars." She smiled at the memory of a Model T that had elicited a story about one of his cousins driving up a mountain-side backward because the engine had only been strong enough in reverse. "Even though we all know cars aren't my passion, I learned more about him in that one week-end than I have...*ever*, really."

He'd thought he was going to die—late at night, alone in his office. And it had made him change direction, hadn't it? Forced him to realize a factory couldn't give hugs or bake your favorite cookies or help you out when you were elderly and in need of some genuine TLC or a trip down memory lane.

"We've even been having phone calls and video-link chats since I left. Every day."

Bea nodded. Impressed now. "Well, if those two hounds of yours are anything to go by, it'll be a successful business in no time. Who knows? I might need one of those itty-bitty handbag assistance dogs to keep me chirpy!"

"Ooh! That's their specialty. Want a display?" Without waiting for an answer, she signaled directions at her specially trained pooches, "Come on, pups! Bedtime for Bea!"

Fran was rewarded with a full peal of Beatrice's giggles when the dogs went up on their hind legs on either side of the bed and pulled at the soft duvet until it was right up to her chin.

Snuggled up under her covers, Bea turned her kind eyes toward Fran. "*Grazie*, Francesca. You're the best. Mamma has promised caffe latte and your favorite *brioche con cioccolata* if we head over to the palazzo tomorrow morning."

"I'll be up early, so don't worry about me. I'll just grab something from this enormous fruit bowl before I shoot off." She feigned trying to lift the huge bowl and failing. "Better save my back. I've got to be there at nine. Fit and well!"

"At Clinica Mont di Mare?"

"Aha! I *knew* I'd get something from you beyond the sat-nav coordinates!"

Bea gave her a sidelong glance, then shook her head. "All I'm going to say is keep an open mind."

"Sounds a bit scary."

Bea gave her hand a squeeze. "Of all the people in the world, I know you're the best one for this particular job."

"Thanks, friend."

Fran fought the tickle of tears in her throat. Bea was her absolute best friend and she trusted her implicitly. The fact Bea was still speaking to her after today's debacle made her heart squeeze tight.

"*Un bacione.*" She dropped a kiss on her friend's forehead and gave her hand a final squeeze before heading to her own bedroom and climbing into the antique wrought iron–framed bed.

"Freda, come! Covers!" *Might as well get as much practice in as possible.*

The fluffy Bernese mountain dog padded over, did as she had been bid, then received a big ol' cuddle. Fran adored Freda, with her big brown eyes. The three-year-old dog was ever patient, ever kind. In contrast to the other full-of-beans dog she'd brought along.

"Edison! Come, boy!"

The chocolate Lab lolloped up to the side of the bed to receive his own cuddle, before flopping down in a contented pile of brown fur alongside Freda.

The best of friends. Just like her and Bea. It would be so hard to say goodbye.

Never mind. Tomorrow was a new beginning.

Exactly what she needed after a certain someone's face had been burned into her memory forever.

"You and I will never be friends."

Luca's hardened features pinged into her mind's eye. No matter the set of his jaw, she'd seen kindness in his eyes. Disbelief at what was happening. And resignation. A trinity of emotions that had pulled at her heartstrings and then yanked hard, cinching them in a tight noose. No matter how foul he'd been, she knew she would always feel compassion for him. Always wonder if he'd found someone worthy of his love.

CHAPTER THREE

"*How* much?" Luca's jaw clenched tight. He was barely able to conceal his disbelief. Another *five million* to get a swathe of family suites prepared?

He looked at the sober-faced contractor. He was the best, and his family had worked with the Montovano family for years. In other words, five million was a steal.

Five million he didn't have, thanks to his father's late nights at the poker table. Very nice poker tables, in the French Riviera's most exclusive casinos. Casinos where losing was always an option.

Luca's eyes flicked up to the pure blue sky above him. Now that his father was pushing piles of chips up there, somewhere in the heavenly hereafter, it wasn't worth holding on to the anger anymore. The bitterness.

His gaze realigned with the village—his inheritance... his millstone. Finding peace was difficult when he had a paraplegic niece to care for and a half-built clinic he was supposed to open in a week's time.

Basta! He shook off the ill will. Nothing would get in the way of providing for Pia. Bringing her every happiness he could afford. Be it sunshine or some much-needed savings—he would give her whatever he had. After the losses she'd suffered...

"Dottore?" The contractor's voice jarred him back into the moment.

"Looks like we're going to have to do it in phases, Piero. *Mi perdoni.*"

Luca didn't even bother with a smile—they both knew it wouldn't be genuine—and shook hands with the disappointed contractor. They walked out to the main gate, where he had parked. Luca remained in the open courtyard as the van slowly worked its way along the kilometer-long bridge that joined the mountaintop village to the fertile seaside valley below.

He took in a deep breath of air—just now hinting at all the wildflowers on the brink of appearing. It was rare for him to take a moment like this—a few seconds of peace before heading back into the building site that needed to be transformed into an elite rehabilitation clinic in one week's time.

He scanned the broad valley below him. Where the hell was this dog specialist? Time was money. Money he didn't have to spare. Not that Canny Canines was charging him. Bea had said something about fulfilling pro bono quotas and rescue dogs, but it hadn't sat entirely right with him. He might have strained the seams of his bag of ducats to the limit, but he wasn't in the habit of accepting charity. Not yet anyway.

The jarring clang of a scaffolding rail reverberated against the stone walls of the medieval village along with a gust of blue language. Luca's fists tightened. He willed it to be the sound of intention rather than disaster. There was no time for mistakes—even less for catastrophe.

Sucking in another deep breath, Luca turned around to face the arched stone entryway that led into the renamed "city." Microcity, more like. Civita di Montovano di Marino. His family's name bore the legacy of a bustling medieval village perched atop this seaside mountain—once thriving in the trades of the day, but now left to fade away to nothing after two World Wars had shaken nearly every family from its charitable embrace.

Just another one of Italy's innumerable ghost towns—barely able to sustain the livelihood of one family, let alone the hundred or so who had lived there so many years ago.

But in one week's time all that would change, when the Clinica Mont di Mare opened its doors to its first five patients. All wheelchair bound. All teenagers. Just like his niece. Only, unlike his niece, *they* all had parents. Families willing to dedicate their time and energy to trying rehabilitation one more time when all the hospitals had said there was no more hope.

A sharp laugh rasped against his throat. After the accident, that was exactly what the doctors at the hospital working with Pia had said. "She'll just have to resign herself to having little to no strength."

Screw that.

Montovanos didn't resign themselves to anything. They fought back. *Hard.*

His hand crept up to the thin raised line of his scar and took its well-traveled route from chin to throat. A permanent reminder of the promise he'd made to his family to save their legacy.

"Zio! Are they here yet?"

Luca looked up and smiled. Pia might not be his kid, but she had *his* blood pumping through her veins. Type A positive. Two liters' worth. Montovano di Marino blood. She was a dead ringer for her mother—his sister—but from the way she was haphazardly bumping and whizzing her way along the cobbled street instead of the wheelchair-ready side path to get to their favorite lookout site, he was pretty sure she'd inherited her bravura from him.

Pride swelled in him as he watched her now—two years after being released from hospital—surpassing each of his expectations with ease.

Breathless, his niece finally arrived beside him. "Move over, Zio Luca. I want to see when she gets here."

"What makes you so sure the trainer is a she?"

"Must be my teenage superpowers." Pia smirked. "And also Bea told me it was a she. Girl power!"

Another deep hit of pride struck him in the chest as he watched her execute a crazy three-point turn any Paralympian would have been hard-pressed to rival and then punch up into the morning sunshine, shouting positive affirmations.

"Never let her down. You're all she has now."

The words pounded his conscience as if he'd heard them only yesterday. His sister's last plea before her fight for survival had been lost.

His little ray of sunshine.

A furnace blast of determination was more like it.

Pia wanted—*needed*—to prove to herself that she could do everything on her own. Her C5 vertebra fracture might have left her paralyzed from the waist down, but it hadn't crushed her spirits as she'd powered through the initial stages of recovery at the same time as dealing with the loss of her parents and grandparents all in one deadly car crash. She had even spoken of training for the Paralympics.

And then early-onset rheumatoid arthritis had thrown a spanner in the works. Hence the dog.

They both scanned the approaching roads. One from the north, the other from the south and their own road—a straight line from the *civita* to the sea, right in the middle.

There was the usual collection of delivery vehicles and medical staff preparing the facility for its opening. And inspectors. Endless numbers of inspectors.

He was a doctor, for heaven's sake—not a bureaucrat.

"Just think, Pia...in one short week that road and this sky will be busy with arriving patients. Ambulances, helicopters..."

She let out a wistful sigh. "Friends!"

"Patients," he reminded her sternly, lips twitching against the smile he'd rather give.

"I know, Uncle Luca. But isn't it part of the Clinica Mont di Mare's ethos that rehab covers all the bases. And that means having friends—like me!"

"Remember, *chiara*, they won't all be as well-adjusted and conversation starved as you."

He gave her plaits a tug, only to have his hand swatted away. She was sixteen. Too old for that sort of thing. Too young to find him interesting 24/7. Having other teens here would be good for her.

"They're all in wheelchairs, right?"

"You know as well as I do they are. And thank you for being a guinea pig for all the doctors here in advance of their coming."

"Anything for Mont di Mare!" Pia's face lit up, then just as quickly clouded. "Do you think they'll try to take my dog? The other patients, I mean? What if they need the dog more than I do?"

Luca shook his head. "No. Absolutely not. This is solely for *you*."

"What if they get jealous and want one, too?"

"That's a bridge to cross further down the line, Pia. Besides," he added gently, "they'll have their families with them."

"I have *you*!" Pia riposted loyally.

"And I have you." He reached out a hand and she met it for a fist bump—still determined to make him hip.

Hard graft for Pia, given everything he'd been dealing with over the past few months in the lead-up to opening the clinic. Endless logistics. Paint samples. Cement grades. Accessibility ramps. Safety rails. And the list went on. It was as if he was missing a part of himself, not being able to practice medicine.

It's what your family would have wanted. You're doing it for them. Medicine will wait.

"Do you think that's her?" Pia's voice rose with excitement.

In the distance they could see a sky blue 4x4 coming along the road from the north, with a telltale blinking light. It was turning left.

"Can't you remember anything about her at all?" Pia looked up at him, eyes sparkling with excitement.

"Sorry, *amore*. Beatrice didn't say much. Just said it was a friend she'd stake our own friendship on."

"Wow! Beatrice is an amazing friend. That means a lot. Not like—" Pia stopped herself and grimaced an apology. "I mean, Marina was never really very nice anyway! You deserve better."

He grunted. There wasn't much to say on the matter. Not anymore. His thoughts were all for Bea and her privacy. He'd offered her a cottage up here at Mont di Mare, but she'd said she needed some serious alone time.

"Do you know what Dr. Murro and I called Marina?" Pia asked, a mischievous smile tweaking at the edges of her sparkle-glossed lips.

He shook his head. "Do I *want* to know?"

"Medusa!" She put her hands up beside her head and turned them into a tangle of serpents, all the while making creepy snake faces.

"Charming, *chiara*. Next time you go to the gym to work with Dr. Murro, please do tell him that perhaps a bit less chat about my defunct love life and a splash more work might be in order."

"Zio!" Pia widened her big puppy-dog eyes. "We can't help it if she was horrible."

Luca gave one of her plaits another playful tug. Just what a man needed. To find out that no one liked his girl-friend all along. Then again...being upset about Marina was pretty much the last thing on his mind. Making the clinic a running, functioning entity was most important.

Six months. That was how far what little money he had left would last before the bank made good on their promise to repossess what had been under his family's care for generations.

Pia shrugged unapologetically, then pulled the pair of binoculars she always had looped around her neck up to her eyes, to track the car that was still making its way toward the turnoff to Mont di Mare.

"I hope Freda looks exactly like she did in the pic-tures Bea forwarded. And Edison. He's *definitely* a he, and Freda's a she, but I'm glad the trainer is a she, too."

"Why's that?"

"It'll be nice to have a grown-up friend."

"You have me!"

"I know, but..." Her eyes flicked away from his.

She'd always been so good about making him feel worthy of the enormous role of caring for her. And yet at moments like these...he knew there were gaps to be filled.

"It'll be nice to have a girl to talk to about...you know...*things*."

Luca looked away. Of *course* she could do with a woman in her life. Someone to fill even a small portion of the hole left when her mother had been killed in that insane accident. A massive truck hurtling toward them from the other side of the tunnel with nowhere else to go...

"Zio! I think I see Freda!"

"Who's Freda?"

"Freda's the *dog*!"

"Right."

"And it *is* a her! She's a *her*!"

"Who? The dog?"

"The *trainer*!"

Pia was clapping with excitement now and Luca couldn't help but crack a smile. His first genuine one in the last twenty-four hours.

"*Zio!* Comb your hair. She's almost here!"

Luca laughed outright. Fat lot of good a comb would do with the rest of him covered in sawdust and paint.

A far cry from his Armani-suited and booted days at his consultancy in Rome. The one none of his colleagues had been able to believe he'd just up and leave for a life in the hinterlands. He wouldn't have wished the life lessons he'd had to learn that night on anyone. His cross to bear. The suits were moth food as far as he was concerned.

He tugged both hands through his hair and messed it up werewolf-style.

"Suitable?"

Pia gave his "makeover" the kind of studious inspection to which only a sixteen-year-old could add gravitas, then rolled her eyes.

"It's not *my* fault if you're a fashion plate," he teased.

"I'm trying to save you from yourself," Pia shot back. "What if she's a beautiful blonde and you fall in love?"

"Nice try, Pia. I'm officially off the market."

"Officially off your rocker, more like," she muttered with an eye roll. "Look! They're turning onto the bridge!"

He spotted the vehicle, then looked out beyond the road and took in the sparkle of the sun upon the Adriatic Sea. Italy's most famed coastline. Croatia and Montenegro were somewhere out there in the distance. Dozens of ports where the world's billionaires parked their superyachts. The price tag of just one of those would have him up and running in no time.

He gave himself a short sharp shake. This wasn't the time for self-pity or envy. It was time to prove he was worthy of the name he'd been given. The name he hoped would stay on this village he now called home.

"Shall we go and greet our new guest?" Luca flourished a hand in the direction of the approaching vehicle, even though his niece already had the wheels of her chair in motion.

Fran had to remind herself to breathe. Way up there on the hilltop was the most beautiful village she'd ever seen. Golden stone. Archways everywhere. The hillsides were terraced in graduated "shelves." If one could define countless acres of verdant wildflower meadows and a generous sprinkling of olive trees to be the "shelves" of a mountainside.

It was almost impossible to focus on driving, let alone the figures coming into view in the courtyard at the end of the bridge. She rolled down the window to inhale a deep breath of air. Meadow grass. The tang of the sea. The sweetness of fruit ripening on trees.

Heaven.

For the first time in just about forever, Fran wondered how she was going to find the strength to leave.

Was that…? *Wait a minute.*

All the air shot out of her lungs.

Long, lean and dark haired was no anomaly in Italy, but she recognized this particular long, lean, dark-haired man. As she clapped eyes on the tall figure jogging along-side the beaming girl in the wheelchair, her heart rate shot into overdrive.

Fight or flight kicked in like something crazy. Her skin went hot and cold, then hot again. Not that it had *any-thing* to do with the picture-perfect jawline and cheek-bones now squaring off in front of her SUV.

No *wonder* Beatrice had been all mysterious and tight-lipped last night.

Un-freakin'-believable.

Mr. You-and-I-Will-Never-Be-Friends was her new boss.

Chills skittered along her arms as their gazes caught and locked.

From the steely look in his eyes he hadn't exactly erased her from *his* memory either.

From the flip-flop of warmth in her tummy, her body hadn't forgotten all that glossy dark hair, tousled like a lusty he-man ready to drag her into a cave and—

Silver linings, Fran. Think of the silver linings. He hates you, so flirting isn't something you need to worry about.

The dogs were both standing up in the back now, mouths open, tongues hanging out as if smiling in an-ticipation of meeting Pia. Trust *them* to remember they were here to help—not ogle the local talent.

Take a deep breath... One...two...three... Here goes nothing.

She pulled the car up to where the pair were waiting, then jumped out and ran around the back to the dogs. The dogs would be the perfect buffer for meeting—

"Francesca."

Gulp! His voice was still all melted chocolate and a splash of whiskey. Or was it grappa because they were in Italy? Whatever. It was all late-night radio and she liked it. Precisely the reason to pretend she didn't by saying absolutely nothing.

"We meet again."

Mmm-hmm. All she could do was nod. Luca had looked a treat in his fancy-schmancy suit yesterday, but now, with a bit of sawdust… *Mmm.* The sleeves of his chambray shirt were rolled up enough to show forearms that had done hard graft…and he wore a pair of hip-riding moleskin trousers that looked as if they'd seen their fair share of DIY…

Mamma mia!

Of all the completely gorgeous, compellingly enigmatic Italians needing an assistance dog for his…

"Allow me to introduce my niece, Pia."

Fran shook herself out of her reverie.

Niece! Nieces were nice.

"Yes! Pia—of course." She swept a few stray wisps of hair behind her ear and turned her full attention on the teenager whose smile was near enough splitting her face in two. "I bet you're far more interested in meeting these two than me."

They all turned to face the back of her SUV, where two big furry heads were panting away in anticipation of meeting their new charge. Fran deftly unlocked the internal cage after commanding the two canines to sit.

"If you'd just back your chair up a bit, Pia. They are both really excited to meet you."

"Both?" Luca's voice shuddered down her spine.

"Yes, both," she answered as solidly as she could. "Not everyone gets off on the right foot when they first meet."

She lifted her gaze to meet his.

Luca's eyebrow quirked.

"Is that so? I thought dogs were instinctive about knowing a good match."

"*Dogs* are," Fran parried, with a little press and push of her lips. "People sometimes need a second chance to get things right."

Luca's eyebrow dipped, then arced again, and just when she was expecting a cutting remark she saw it— the kindness she'd knew she'd seen lurking somewhere in those smoky brown eyes of his.

"Zio! Leave Francesca alone. I want to see the dogs!"

Grateful for the reprieve from this verbal fencing, Fran turned her focus to a starry-eyed Pia as her eyes pinged from one dog to the other.

"Aren't they a bit…big?" Luca stepped forward, his presence feeling about a thousand times more powerful than either dog did to Fran.

"Zio Luca! No!" Pia protested. "They are perfect. Both of them!"

"She's actually right." Fran shrugged an apology. "When Bea explained that your village offered unique challenges in the navigating department, I thought a mountain dog would be perfect."

"You mean the big one?" Pia pointed at Freda, the Bernese.

"I sure do." She shot a glance toward Luca, who had moved back from his protective position but still held a wary look in his eye.

She always forgot that to a person who wasn't used to dogs a Bernese could seem enormous. *Baby pony* was an oft-heard phrase when mountain dog "virgins" first saw them.

"Come along, Freda. Let's say hello to Pia."

"Surely Labs are more reliable. In terms of charac-ter." Luca stepped forward again, just managing to slot himself between Fran and Pia before she asked the dog to jump out.

Fran bit down hard on the inside of her cheek before replying. "Both dogs are extremely gentle and come with my one hundred percent guarantee."

"And what exactly is *that* worth?" Luca arced an eye-brow, daring her to name a number.

Fran's blood boiled. She wasn't here to prove herself to anyone. She was here to help. How *dare* he put her to some sort of ridiculous test of worth?

"I'll leave right now, if you think that's what's best. But I can guarantee that by the end of the day you will see a change in your niece's life. And as it is Pia's life we're talking about, perhaps *she* should be the one who is deciding."

They both turned to look at her, but when his niece opened her mouth to interject, Luca held out a hand to stop her.

"As her guardian, I make all the decisions for Pia's welfare."

"As an experienced trainer, I know you'd be making a mistake by turning me away."

Luca's inky, dark eyes stayed glued to hers, his face completely immovable. She felt as if she was clashing with a gladiator. One false move and—*crack!*—down she'd go. It didn't stop her from wanting to reach out and touch that salt-and-pepper stubble of his, though. Soft or scratchy...?

"You and I will never be friends."

"So?" Defiance saturated Fran's posture, but she didn't care. "Are you happy for me to unload them? Start bring-ing some empowerment to your niece's life?"

Without a backward glance Fran quickly clipped leads onto the dogs, and silently commanded them to jump down, approach Pia and present their paws for a handshake.

Pia laughed, delightedly taking each dog's paw for a shake, then giving their heads an adoring pat.

"Zio! *Per favore!* Can they all stay forever?" Pia's plaits flipped from one shoulder to the next as she looked between the two dogs and then beamed up at Fran as if she were a fairy godmother, complete with a magic wand. Which was nice. It was good to have someone rooting for her when the other person looked as if he'd happily tip her off the side of the mountain.

Fran turned toward Luca and crossed her arms. "Two against one?"

"Four against one," Pia said, then quickly tacked on in a gentler plea. "If that's okay, Zio? Can they at least stay until the end of the day?"

Luca's hands slipped to his hips as if he were reaching for invisible holsters. A small gust of wind rustled his already tousled hair. Off in the distance, Fran saw a rising plume of dust, as if a band of horses and *banditos* were heading their way to intervene. A showdown at dawn—minus the weapons and the sunrise.

"I promise you'll see a difference. In an hour, even."

Luca's eyelids lowered to half-mast as his glance skidded away from her toward the dogs and then back to her.

Too much? *Oh, jinks.* How was she going to tell her father she'd messed up Canny Canines before she'd even had a chance to begin? Yes, she wanted to go back—but not with her proverbial tail between her legs.

"*Per favore*, Francesca." Luca affected a courtly bow, though the charm didn't quite make it to his eyes. "My niece seems to want to give you a tour. Please. Allow us to show you around our humble abode."

He stood up to his full height, brow furrowed tight at the bridge of his aquiline nose.

"Then we'll talk."

CHAPTER FOUR

FRAN'S GAZE CAUGHT with Luca's. If he wasn't being sincere, she was out of here.

What? And run home to Daddy a failure before you've even begun?

She forced herself to look deep into the mahogany darkness of his irises and seek answers. He didn't look away this time. He held his ground—eyes glued to hers—as if he knew what she was looking for.

Somewhere between the crackle of "I dare you to fail" and the burn of "she's all I've got," Fran found what she needed. The answer. How she knew that Luca was hiding a good man deep within that flinty exterior of his was beyond her—but she did.

"Luca, I just wanted—"

Of all the times for her backside to vibrate!

"Can you excuse me for just a moment?" Fran tugged her cell phone out of her back pocket, instructed the dogs to stay with Pia and Luca, then scooted off to the far end of the village's central plaza, where their tour of the "humble abode" was just wrapping up.

"Beatrice?" She didn't wait for a reply. "You are truly the evilest friend I have ever had the privilege of knowing."

Bea's wicked cackle trilled down the line. "I guess you've met the baron, then?"

"The baron?"

"Luca. Il Barone Montovano di Marino. Didn't I tell you he was a baron?"

She'd been at her lippiest, sassiest best with a *baron*?

"Princess Beatrice, you know blinking well you didn't tell me *anything*! And, yes. Since you ask, we *have* met, formed an instant kinship, become blood siblings and vowed to be the absolute best of friends forever and ever."

There was a beat.

Too sarcastic?

"Well, make sure you use an antiseptic wipe. It would be a shame if your new BFF had to chop off your finger because of a case of sepsis," Bea said without a hint of apology. Then she added, "I *knew* you two would get along."

"Yeah. Like water and oil."

"Oh, don't be ridiculous. He enjoys being a baron as much as you love being sole heiress to Martinelli Motors, so cool your jets. You two will hit it off. Mark my words."

Hmm… Time would have to be the arbiter on that one.

"Everything okay with you?"

"What do you think of Mont di Mare? Pretty impressive, eh?"

"Nice dodge, my friend." Fran tugged at her ponytail before deftly knotting it into a bun at the base of her neck. "Tell me you're all right and then I'll tell you how meeting Luca really went. Thunder and lightning are your two clues."

She glanced across at Luca and her eyes went wide. He was kneeling beside the dogs, calling out half-hearted protests as Edison gave him a good old-fashioned face cleaning while Freda kept trying to put her paws on his shoulders for a hug. Pia's eyes were lit up bright. Not so brooding and glowering after all, then…

"Everything's fine, Fran. I'm planning an escape under the cover of darkness!"

Hearing Bea add melodramatic dum-dah-dum-dum noises was all the reassurance Fran needed. She was smarting, but she'd be fine.

"Any clues about where you're headed? I hear Transylvania's nice this year."

"Ha-ha. Vampires aren't my style."

"*No one* has your amount of style. Or class," Fran insisted.

"No need to fluff my ego, Fran. I'm going to be fine."

"You're amazing, Bea. Seriously. I don't think I'd be as calm and collected in your shoes."

"It's…it's a relief, really. My only goal is to get through the next few months with no paparazzi. Yours should be to get Luca to cook his stuffed pumpkin flowers for you. *Delicioso!*"

"He cooks?"

"Like a dream."

Fran grinned at the sound of Beatrice kissing the tips of her fingers.

"And just remember, Frannie, his bark is worse than his bite. He's a pussycat, really,"

Fran muttered a few disbelieving words to the contrary, but something in her fluttered as she caught sight of Luca trying—and failing—to get the dogs to stop chasing him.

Maybe he was just taking out his frustration about Marina on her. He wouldn't be the first man she'd met who'd dealt with a broken heart by taking it out on her.

Dads are different, Fran.

Besides. Something told her Luca wasn't exactly brokenhearted about Marina.

"Steel exterior. Molten heart," Beatrice insisted. "You two'll be friends before you know it."

Humph. Doubtful.

She looked over and saw Luca, lying flat on his back, with the dogs appearing to give him some sort of chest compressions. Seeing him all silly and smiley made him...

"Beautiful..."

"He *is* a hottie, isn't he?" Bea teased.

"The place—not the man," Fran swiftly corrected.

"As I said," her friend teased, "time will change all that. You'll be fine. Just remember—Luca's the hawk... Pia's his fledgling. She's his number one concern. You get that right, your summer will be golden."

Fran shot a look up to the pure blue sky, hoping there was someone up there watching out for her. She had a feeling she'd need all the help she could get this summer.

"You *sure* you don't want to come up here to Mont di Mare? Luca told me he'd offered you an invitation."

"No, *chiara*. I'm all right. Just be there on the end of the phone if I need you?"

"Always."

"*Un bacione*, Fran. *Ciao!*"

"*Ciao, ciao!* Be safe."

She clicked the phone off and cast a final wish up to the heavens that Bea would find somewhere beautiful and private to heal. When she dropped her gaze, her eyes met and clashed with Luca's. Goose bumps ran across her arms as she watched the shutters slam down, cloaking the warm, loving man she'd just caught a glimpse of.

Never you mind, Il Barone. I'll show you everything I'm made of and then some.

"Bea." Fran held up the phone, toward him, as if it would prove their mutual friend had been on the line.

"Ending your friendship after yesterday's debacle?"

From the sharp intake of breath and the hollowing of Francesca's cheeks Luca knew he'd pushed it too far. Been too brusque. *Again.*

"Quite the opposite," she replied evenly, her eyes darting about the courtyard until they lit on some bloodred roses. A beautiful contrast to her honey-tanned skin. She bent forward, then stopped herself, giving him a sidelong glance. "I trust there aren't any rules against smelling the roses here?"

Her blue eyes widened, daring him to say otherwise.

He looked away as she called the dogs to heel, only to catch a don't-be-so-grumpy glare from his niece. A sharp reminder of who he was doing this for. All of it. When life ripped your entire family away from you except for one precious soul you cherished it. And he was making a hash of that, as well. Too out of practice. Too many of his earlier years spent being intent on the wrong goals. If he'd known the learning curve to making things right would be so hard…

He'd still be doing it. Even if it meant putting up with Little Miss Ray of Sunshine for the next two months. Pia seemed smitten and that was what counted.

Despite himself, Luca's eyes were drawn to Francesca like a feline to catnip. The fullness of her lips was darkened to a deep emotional red. Not a speck of any other makeup. Jeans and a baseball shirt that teased at the edges of her shoulders. Her blond hair was pulled back from her face in a thick ponytail that swished between her shoulder blades when she walked. Not that he'd been watching her closely… Her shoes were practical leather ankle boots, similar to the boots horsey types wore. Funny… He could easily picture her riding a horse along the mountain trails. Something he and his sister had often done, disappearing for hours at a time, stuffing themselves with wild berries and drinking straight from the mountain streams.

Those days were gone now. Long gone. Just as Francesca's fripperies from yesterday's wedding had all but disappeared. No more soft pink nail polish. No eye shadow, mascara. All of it cleared away to show off her distinct natural beauty. The countryside suited her. Mont di Mare suited her—as if an Old Master had painted her there and just changed her clothing with the passage of time…

"Freda. Edison." Fran commanded the dogs to sit with a gesture, shot Luca an over-the-shoulder wait-for-it-look, then a mischievous grin to Pia. She whipped out her fingers pistol-style and "shot" each of the dogs, who instantly rolled over and played dead.

Pia was consumed by gales of laughter and Fran's lips had parted into a full-fledged smile. One a movie star would have paid a lot for.

"Is there anything *useful* they can do?"

"Zio Luca!" Pia swiped at the air between them. "What *has* got into you today?"

"I'm just waiting to see if Francesca has something helpful to show us. What was it? An hour, she said, and we'd see a change?"

"She made me laugh," Pia growled.

He opened his mouth to protest. Surely he and Pia had laughed… No. Not so much. Especially in the weeks since the bank had slapped the deadline on him. Six months or *finito*.

"Pia—" Fran took a couple of steps forward "—could I use your binoculars for a minute?"

"*Si*, of course." She untangled the strap from her plaits and handed them to Fran.

Without a second glance at Luca, Fran took a scan around the plaza.

"Can you distract the dogs for a minute?"

Pia obliged as Fran jogged over to a small olive tree and hung the binoculars on a low branch, then jogged back.

"Freda." She signaled to Pia's neck. "Where are the binoculars?"

Luca watched wordlessly as the dog took a quick sniff of Pia, did a quick zigzag around the courtyard, abruptly loped over to the olive tree, spotted and tugged down the binoculars by their strap, then padded back, offering the binoculars to a delighted Pia.

"Impressive," he acquiesced. "But hardly a life changer."

Fran pushed her lips forward into a little moue. One that said, *You ain't seen nothin' yet, cowboy.*

He folded his arms and rocked his weight back onto his heels. *Go on*, his stance said. *Prove it.*

A flare of irritation lit up her eyes, bringing a smile to his lips. He got to her as much as she got to him. A Mutual Aggravation Society.

In quick succession Fran ran both dogs through a number of tasks. She had Pia wheel around the courtyard, dropping various items. The dogs picked them all up. They found exits from the courtyard on command. The dogs pushed the wheelchair from one point to another, navigating it around the low-slung branches of the various fruit trees dappling the area.

Fran slipped each dog into a harness and had them take turns pulling Pia on various routes around the courtyard, stopping at one point to pick up a set of keys that had slipped from Luca's pocket. The display culminated in each dog barreling out of the courtyard and returning two minutes later, triumphant, with their water bowls tucked in their mouths, and then dropping them at Fran's feet.

She turned to him, arms crossed in satisfaction. "Proof enough for you?" The arc in her eyebrow dared him to say otherwise.

He made a noncommittal noise, his eyes glued to Fran's, as sharp hit after hit of connection exploded in his chest. He rammed the sensations to the background. Work and Pia. His only two concerns. Francesca brought chaos in her wake. She teased too cruelly at his instinctive urges to pull her in close and taste exactly what those full lips of hers—

"They're *amazing*, Zio! Aren't they amazing? We should get dogs for all the patients! Wouldn't that be just the best?" Pia reeled off her praises, failing to notice the crackle of electricity surging between her uncle and Fran.

He took a step back to break the connection. "Bravo, Francesca." Luca gave a stilted clap, trying to ignore his niece's ebullient response. "I'm sorry to bring the display to an end, but I'm afraid my niece has to spend some time with her tutor."

"It's English lessons, Zio. I could practice with Francesca, *si*?"

"No," he answered in his most pronounced Italian accent. The role of cantankerous uncle was coming to him a bit too fluidly, but needs must. Their world had mayhem enough without a canine-training Mary Poppins running around the place with fairy dust and moonbeams.

Although it was better than Marina's preference, that the village be revamped into an exclusive hotel. Little wonder she'd chosen Marco. He had glitz and glamour down to a T.

Pia gave an exasperated sigh but turned her wheelchair toward the arched stone passageway that led to their

ANNIE O'NEIL   57

private quarters before abruptly spinning around. "Can they—will the dogs be able to come with me?"

"Absolutely." Fran nodded with a quick backward glance to check that it was okay with Luca.

He nodded.

"They are *your* buddies now. Freda is the one I thought might best suit your needs, but it's a good idea to spend time with both of them. We can meet later and talk about things you specifically need help with and start to set up a training routine. Sound good?"

"Cramp!" Pia screamed suddenly, her hands seizing into gnarled fists. "Cramp!"

Without a second glance Fran was on her knees in front of Pia, cupping her hands together, kneading one, then the other, tension knotting her brow as tears formed in Pia's eyes.

"Do you have any heat wraps?" She glanced up at Luca, completely oblivious to the shock in his eyes.

"Let me." Luca reached out to take his niece's slender hands, noting as he did the expert efficiency with which Fran massaged Pia's fingers.

"I'm a physiotherapist. It's fine," Fran said.

"Certified by the University of Life?"

"Harvard," she snapped back. "Good enough for you?" She continued massaging Pia's hands. "You'd be best getting those heat wraps."

"*I* decide what's best for my niece—not you."

"Zio, *please*," Pia pleaded through her tears. "Francesca is doing fine. Please can you get the wraps?"

"I've got a sock filled with rice in my car, if there's a microwave nearby. You just throw the sock in for a—"

"I have appropriate heat wraps. I just—" *I just don't want to leave her with you.* Though unspoken, the words crackled in the air between them.

Francesca continued her fluid movements, but turned her head to face him. "She will be safe with me," she said, more solidly than he'd thought possible. "I will take care of her."

He looked at his niece, her features crumpled in pain, and made the decision.

He ran.

The sooner he left, the sooner he would be back.

A dog trainer *and* a physio? There was a story there. But it was one that would have to wait.

A few minutes later he returned, astonished to see Pia's face wreathed in smiles, her hands lodged in the Bernese mountain dog's "armpits."

"Stand-in heat pads." Fran shrugged, pushing up from her knees at the foot of Pia's wheelchair.

"Rendering these unnecessary?" Luca held up the hot packs he'd already cracked so that they'd be ready for action.

"Sorry." Fran shrugged again and turned to her dogs with a grin, seemingly oblivious to the thousands of dark thoughts that had run through his head as he'd raced to the clinic, pawed through the storage cupboards, then raced back only to find his efforts had been for naught.

"I brought you some electrolyte water, too, Pia. In case you were dehydrated."

"Is she on any medication?"

Luca's eyes widened. "I have brought her what she needs. Pia's on a couple of things for her paraplegia, but other than that has made the choice not to start on any medication until she absolutely has to."

"Right *here*, Zio Luca. No need to talk about me as if I'm invisible!"

"I've got some great cream recipes we can make up that might help," Fran said to Pia, barely acknowledging

Luca. "I bet there are loads of medicinal herbs and flowers growing out there. The dogs and I can forage for you!"

"That'd be great!" Pia enthused.

"Here." Luca took his niece's hands in his and wove the heat pad between them. "Better?"

Pia nodded, then turned away.

"Fran?"

Luca watched as Pia looked up at Fran with a shy look he rarely saw from his niece.

"I'm glad you're here."

"Me, too," Fran replied straight away, then looked up, her azure eyes meeting Luca's as powerfully as a bolt of lightning. There was a connection there. A vivid, primal, deep-seated connection.

One he was going to have to bury in order to survive.

Once Pia had left, her hands wrapped around a heat pad, the tutor in control of the wheelchair and the dogs trotting merrily behind, Fran and Luca eyed each other warily.

A lion and a tigress vying for supremacy. Or a truce?

Fran broke the silence "It's very beautiful up here."

"Far too much room for improvement," he countered, wincing when he saw she'd taken it personally.

Luca put on his "bright" voice, knowing it would sound a bit strangled, but he wasn't ready for making nice with Fran. Might not ever be.

"Shall we get you and your things to your quarters?"

"If that means I'm staying?"

He shot her a noncommittal look. "It's a long walk. Plenty of time to change my mind."

The incident with Pia had shaken him. He was his niece's warrior—her defense against the countless aches and pains she'd had to tackle and overcome since the ac-

cident. Getting her an assistance dog was one thing. Seeing her reach to someone else for help...

It hurt.

More than leaving his exclusive reconstructive surgery
clinic in Rome to bring his niece here had hurt. More than
discovering, once he'd arrived, that his father had leveraged Mont di Mare to within an inch of its life. More
than staring daily at the scar he would never fix, keeping
it as a reminder—a vivid, daily reminder—of the prom-
ises he'd made to do his very best for Pia.

"Hello? Luca?" Fran was waving her hand in front
of his face. "You've obviously got things on your mind,
and about *this* much patience for me—" She pinched at a
smidgen of air, then crushed it between her fingers. "So
if you'd just point the way, I'm sure I can find it myself."

"No, you can't."

He bit back a smile as Fran bridled at his pronounce-
ment.

"I happen to have a very good sense of direction."

"I'm sure you do, but we haven't put any signs up on
the doors, so it'll be tricky for you to find your cottage."

"Cottage?" Fran's eyes widened in delight as she
tugged a couple of medium-sized tote bags out of the
truck onto the stone plaza.

She did that a lot. As if everything new was a pleasure
rather than a burden. Each corner turned was a moment
of thrilling excitement rather than full of the dread that
enveloped him whenever a foreman or a staffer headed
his way with a purposeful gait and an I-need-to-bend-
your-ear-for-a-minute look in his eye.

Fatigue. That was all it was. The clinic was a massive
project. The ramifications of failing were too weighty
to bear.

"Shall we?"

Fran gave him a wary look, shifting her weight so that her crossed arms formed a protective shield. "Look. I know we didn't get off to a very good start yesterday."

"That would be putting it mildly." They were past niceties. She might as well know she could count him out of her new-friend posse.

"I'm really, truly, incredibly sorry about what happened, but—no offense—I'm much sorrier for Bea, who has to deal with all the mess left by that ratbag fiancé of hers."

"Ratbag?" Luca quirked an eyebrow. Honesty. He liked that in a woman.

"Ratbag," Beatrice replied solidly.

"At last." He picked up one of her bags from the ground where she'd let them drop. "Something we agree on."

"Phew!" She gave a melodramatic swipe of her brow before picking up the other tote bag and running along after him. "And I just want to say I am genuinely grateful for the chance to experiment up here with Pia and the dogs."

"Experiment?" Luca dropped the bag and turned on her. "I don't have time for *experiments*! I need exacting, perfect, unrelentingly driven, skill-based superiority in *everything*. In *everyone* who comes through these gates! Doctors, nurses, cleaners and, most of all, *you*! You are the one person I'm relying on most to help!"

Fran's jaw dropped open, her eyes widening as the stream of vitriol continued.

As the words poured out and he felt his gestures grow more emphatic Luca abruptly clamped his lips tight and stuffed his fists into his pockets. Baring his heart to Bea in the form of this tirade was as good as…as good as showing his hand.

He almost laughed at the irony. His poker face was as

poor as his father's. His father had lost the family fortune. Had *he* just lost Pia's shot at a bit of independence?
Some much-deserved fun?

Extraordinarily, Francesca just stood there. Dry-eyed.
Patient. Listening to his tongue-lashing as if in fact he
was calmly explaining that he was terribly sorry, but he'd
been under tremendous pressure owing to the imminent
launch of the clinic and, as a result, his concern for his
niece and her welfare was escalating. That it pained him
to admit it, but he needed support. He needed *her.*

"Feel better?" Fran finally asked after the silence between them had grown heavy with expectation.

"Not really," Luca answered, furious with himself for
letting down his guard. He reached for her bags again.
"Let's get on with this, shall we? I've already wasted too
much time today."

Fran held her ground. "I want you to know I'm willing to stake everything I am on those dogs."

"And what *is* that exactly? Beyond, of course, wedding
whistle-blower and circus-trick performer?"

"That's not fair."

"My time is precious, signorina—I'm afraid I didn't
catch your surname."

Fran's eyes narrowed. Her teeth took part of her full
lip captive, unfurling it bit by bit.

"Martinelli."

When she said it, he saw a change in her. A hint of
something he knew *he* saw when he bothered to look at
his own reflection in the mirror. Not the scar. The pain.
The pain that came from no longer being part of something he should have cherished so much more than he
had.

Family.

One simple word that equaled a heady combination

of love, guilt, trying to do better and not getting a single damn thing right.

"Looks like there's a story there," Luca said.

She shrugged.

"Complicated?"

"Very." Her lips pressed forward before thinning into a tight smile.

Luca tipped his chin in understanding. "Looks like we've found *two* things in common."

If there was anyone who grasped *complicated*, it was him.

"Let's cut across here." Luca pointed toward a short covered alley. "It's the long way around."

Fran arched an eyebrow at him.

"I like to get to know my staff."

"I'm not charging you, so technically I'm not staff."

"I can fire you, so technically you *are*. My niece is the single most important person to me in this world. If I'm not happy, you're gone."

Free or not, he wasn't letting just *anyone* get involved with Pia.

"My niece seems to like you. I have yet to be persuaded. With the clinic opening, and no time to look for someone else, I'll give you a chance to prove me wrong."

"And for that I humbly thank you, my lord." An effervescent laugh burbled up and out of Fran's throat as she went into a deep curtsy. "Or is it *Your Excellency*? How *does* one address a baron?"

If he hadn't been so irritated, he would have laughed. She was right to mock him. The arrogance! Since when had he become such a stuck-up prig?

"It's Luca," he said finally, willing himself not to smile. "That's all you need to know."

"Got it." Fran winked, tapping the side of her nose. "Your undercover name."

"Something like that."

He pointed her toward the path they'd need to take to her cottage. Close to his cottage. *Too* close, he realized now. Yet another note for his to-do list: *don't get attached. She'll be gone soon enough.*

CHAPTER FIVE

"DID BEA TELL you anything about me?" Fran asked once they'd walked for a bit in silence, stopping at a bench overlooking the peaks and folds of the surrounding countryside. She focused on a field full of sunflowers. A reminder of all the good she hoped would come of moving back home.

"No. Why?" Luca eyes narrowed, interesting little crinkles fanning out from the corners of his eyes as he tried to figure it out on his own.

"Well, for starters, my full name is Francesca Lisbetta Martinelli." Fran gave him a moment before asking, "Nothing?"

"I've not got all day, Francesca." A flicker of impatience crossed his features.

"Vincente Martinelli... Lui è mio padre."

Saying it in Italian seemed to come more naturally. She and her father spoke it at home. She might as well pronounce her paternity in his native tongue.

"Basta! No? Really?"

A panoply of reaction passed across Luca's face. It was a little bit like watching a short film. Such an interesting face. Not just the scar, which she was aching to touch. There were other stories there. Stories she'd love to hear if only her presence didn't drive him so batty.

"So that makes you…?"

"The daughter of a billionaire."

A flash of understanding lit up his eyes, then disappeared so quickly she thought she'd imagined it.

"And your point is…?" Luca spun his finger in a keep-talking swirl, then gave his watch a sharp tap.

Not the usual reaction. That was nice. Most people wanted to know why she didn't walk around dripping in jewels and designer labels.

"I'm moving home at the end of the summer."

"And…?" Luca's impatience was growing.

"I've not lived there for a long time. Or ever accepted my father's help. But this time…this time he's going to invest in my business."

"The dogs?" Luca's eyebrows lifted.

He obviously thought it was a weird choice, but it wasn't his money, so…

"The point being I've never accepted money from him. *Ever.* And I'm not going home with a fail on my books before I've even started."

Luca blinked, processing that.

"Why are you accepting his help now?"

"Because I want my dad back in my life. And I want him to be proud of me. I believe in what I'm doing this time."

"*This* time?" A flash of concern darkened his features.

"I used to be a physiotherapist. Well, physio and hydrotherapy."

"Why did you give it up?"

She considered him for a moment. He didn't need to know the whole story. Going into business with a "friend" only to discover he'd thought being partners with her meant tapping into her father's wealth.

"One of my patients asked me to help a dog with arthritis. Working with dogs seemed more…"

"Satisfying?" Luca suggested.

"Sounds like the voice of experience," she countered, unwilling to tell Luca how betrayed she'd felt. How hurt. She'd wanted to go to her father, but had felt too ridiculous to confess how foolish she'd been. The last thing she expected from Luca—or anyone—was sympathy. Being an heiress was hardly tragic. Just…*tricky.*

"So you just abandoned your patients? Left on a whim?"

"No. I oversaw their treatment until I could transfer them all to someone I trusted."

"A boyfriend?"

Where had *that* come from?

"My mentor. She took on each and every patient."

"And once you'd shaken off your responsibilities—"

"I didn't shake them off!" Fran protested.

"You left."

"I was young."

"And why should I believe you won't do the same to Pia?"

"You're just going to have to trust me."

Luca's jaw tightened. *Trust.* That was what it was going to boil down to.

"Why should I trust you?"

"I did what was right yesterday, even though it could have cost me the friendship I hold dearest in my heart." Fran's eyes clouded with more emotion than she'd hoped to betray. She swallowed it down and continued, "That, and the second I saw *you* were the person I'd be working for I could've turned the car around and left right then and there. But the dogs seemed excited. They like Pia.

Which makes sense. They seem to like *you*. Which makes less sense. But I trust them. Dogs are loyal."

"Three," Luca said grimly.

"Three?"

"Three things we agree on. Dogs are the only sentient creatures who have any loyalty. Excluding, of course, my niece. If she can stick with me, she can stick with anyone."

"Ah! Finally admitting you're a bit of a Mr. Cranky Pants, then?"

Fran teased at the corner of her T-shirt. Had she overstepped the mark with that one?

"Not a chance, *carina*."

Fran looked up at his change of tone and was caught completely off balance as Luca flashed her a wicked smile.

Santo cielo! A swirl of sparks swept through Fran's tummy, lighting up all sorts of places she'd rather not think about when she was trying to be serious and grown-up. Sort of. Maybe…

"Whatever." She clucked dismissively, feeling a bit more like herself. "Just you wait. Beatrice has assured me we'll be friends. That'll be my summer challenge."

Luca grunted. "We're a long way from friends, *bellissima*. And we're nearly at your cottage." He tipped his head toward a wooden door.

Shame she couldn't convince him to stand there all day. Backlit by the sun. Hair tousled by the gentle breeze. The outline of his body looking rugged and capable. The perfect alpha male to have a summer romance with and then get on with the rest of her life.

As if *that* would ever happen.

"Any final tidbits of wisdom about assistance dogs you want to impart before I drop you off at your cottage?"

"So you're going to let me stay?"

She watched as he processed her question—his teeth biting together, his jaw giving that telltale stress twitch along the line of his scar, his lips parting to demand one last task.

"Give me one word to describe the change you see in your customers once they have a Fran Special."

One word?

"Wait—give me a minute." She scrunched her eyelids tight in order to think and came up blank. In a panic, she looked up into Luca's espresso-dark gaze and it came to her. "Breathtaking."

Just like you, bellissima.

The words popped into Luca's mind and near enough escaped his lips as Fran's blue eyes lit up, her cheeks flushing with pleasure and undiluted pride in what she did.

It was the same sensation *he* felt when a reconstruction surgery had gone to plan. Particularly when a patient picked up a mirror for the first time and, eyes brightening, exclaimed, "It's the old me!" That was far better than the enhancement surgeries that paid the bills. If Mont di Mare could one day do charitable cases, that would be a dream come true.

He shook the thought away. An impossibility right now. A far-off dream.

"So, what's your decision?"

Luca shook his head, temporarily confused. "What decision?"

"Are you going to let me stay—" she swung her thumb toward the village entryway "—or do we have to drag these bags back to my car and pick up the dogs so I can hoof it?"

Pragmatics told him to send her away.

Fran was chaos. He needed peace.

But a splinter of doubt pierced through his more reasoned side.

Perhaps it *wasn't* chaos she brought. Perhaps it was… possibility. And that meant change. Never easy, but sometimes necessary.

The look of glee on his niece's face when she'd seen not only the dogs but Fran had tugged at his sensibilities. Not to mention the sheer expectation on Fran's face now, which was making too great a play on his heartstrings. The strings of the heart he was beginning to realize had never quite regained its usual cheerful cadence since the accident. The very same heart he felt opening, just a sliver, to this ray of joy standing before him. Besides, *he* didn't have to spend time with her. Pia did.

"Si." He gave Fran a quick nod before adding wryly. "Pia might disown me if I say otherwise."

A whoop that might have filled a football stadium flew out of Fran's throat and she immediately launched into some sort of whirling happy dance, the likes of which, he was quite sure, the streets of Mont di Mare had never seen.

Oh, Dio!

Had he *really* just welcomed Hurricane Fran into their lives?

Dance finished, Fran eventually came to a standstill, chest heaving with excitement, eyes alight with the power of that single yes.

"Really?" Endearingly, her voice hit the higher altitudes of her range and her fingers went all pitter-patter happy. "I promise you won't regret it. And when Pia's at school I will *totally* help with painting or putting up

wallpaper or making beds—anything you need. I'll even change bedpans when the patients arrive if it will help."

"We have moved a bit beyond bedpans in terms of patient care."

"Cool." Fran was unfazed. "Whatever the least favorite jobs are, count me in."

He began to shake his head no, but she stopped him with a finger on his lips.

"I won't take no for an answer. You're helping me more than you know, and from what I've gleaned—" they both turned to watch yet another delivery truck begin its way up the bridge toward the clinic "—you have a lot to do. Another pair of hands isn't going to hurt anything, is it? Three years of boarding school has ensured my hospital corners are excellent in the bed-making department."

"How's your grouting?" he asked, in a tone more suited to a master tiler than a doctor doing his best to bring a thousand loose ends together into one beautiful tapestry.

"Unparalleled!" she shot back without the blink of an eye. "My sanding skills are a bit rusty, but I know my way around a mop and bucket something serious."

A sudden urge to pull Fran into his arms seized Luca. If he had Fran on his side she'd no doubt start spreading her pixie dust and turn the entire workload from a burden into an adventure. Why *shouldn't* he have a partner in crime?

Because the bank was threatening to take it all away.

If you'd paid more attention to your father, seen how low he was feeling...

Their gazes connected, meshing in a taut sensation of heightened awareness, powerful currents of electricity surging between the pair of them. Holding them together as one. Sensations he hadn't felt for a long time charged through him, lighting up parts of his body to a wattage he hadn't felt in even longer.

The buzzing of his phone checked the sensations. The raw attraction.

He glanced at the screen.

Work.

The consultant for one of his patients who'd be flying in by helicopter a week from today.

Fun and spontaneity would have to wait.

The first hit of genuine attraction he'd felt in years would have to go untended.

He had bills to pay.

"*Scusi.* I've got to take this."

"Of course." Fran's smile bore the same shade of disappointment he felt in his marrow. "Patients come first."

He took a few steps away, the smile he'd so recently worn eradicated without a trace. "*Si,* Dr. Firenze. How can I help you?"

CHAPTER SIX

THE WEEK HAD passed in a blur. An adrenaline-fueled blur that was about to culminate in the arrival of his first five patients. T minus eighteen hours and counting.

Luca pulled the weights out of their packaging and began lining them up on the rack. These would all be in use soon.

He sat back on his heels and scanned the rehab gym. Gleaming weights machines. Several pairs of handrails ready to bear the weight of patients ready to be put to the test.

The doctor in him itched to get back to work. Not the doctor who'd worn the fancy suits and tended to Rome's image-conscious elite. The doctor who'd retrained at night after working all day with his niece. The doctor who'd poured every last cent he had into getting to this point.

At least Pia and Fran had been so engrossed in working with the dogs that Luca hadn't had to add the guilt of neglecting his niece to everything else he was feeling. And, in fairness to Fran, she'd gone above and beyond being an assistance-dog trainer this past week. Any spare moment she'd had away from Pia and the dogs had, true to her word, been spent doing anything and everything she could to get the clinic to the gleaming, immaculate state of readiness it was in now.

"Are you ready for the big reveal?" Fran appeared in the doorway, a mischievous smile making her look more imp than workhorse.

"Does Pia really need to do this *now*? Half of Mont di Mare still isn't renovated. I haven't checked the patients' rooms or the family quarters yet, and there are still—"

"C'mon!" Fran held up a hand, then arced her arm, waving for him to join her. "This means a lot to her— and I have an idea about the other thing. The unrenovated tidbits."

"How unusual," he answered drily.

Tidbits.

Half the village, more like: ten family houses, ten more patient rooms and the same number again for common rooms and treatment facilities. *Tidbits.* Only an American! He checked himself. Only an *optimist* like Fran would call the amount of work left to be done tidbits. The same projects that buoyed her up near enough pinned him to the ground with worry. What had *possessed* him to turn one of the least disabled-friendly places in the universe into a specialized clinic for disabled people?

Optimism?

Necessity?

"All right." He pushed up from the floor once the final row of weights had been laid out. "Let's hear it, Little Miss Creativity."

"Ha-ha. Very funny, Signor White-Walls-or-Bust." She fluttered her lashes. "It's not *my* fault the spirit of Italy's esteemed relationship with beauty and art courses through my veins and not yours."

Luca watched, unexpectedly transfixed as Fran struck a modeling pose, swooshing her hair up and over one shoulder as she skidded her slender fingers along the length of her athletic figure, eventually coming to rest on her thigh.

He tried to tamp down the flare of heat rising within him.

A lab coat would be most convenient right about now.

He cleared his throat. There were things to do. A clinic to open. This mysterious "reveal" to witness. No doubt another one of Pia's feats with her dogs rather than Francesca reenacting Salome's Dance of the Seven Veils.

He considered the swish of her derriere as she turned to walk down the hall.

Pity.

Where *had* he put those lab coats?

She glanced over her shoulder. "I'll spell out my idea on the way, and you can let me know if it's a yea or a nay by the time we get there." Fran glanced back again, eyes widening as he remained glued to the spot for no apparent reason. "It's our *thing*! Walking, talking, deciding. Remember?"

Just one week together and they had a "thing"? He rolled his eyes.

She dropped him a wink.

A flirtatious wink.

Was that the tip of her tongue peeking out between her teeth, giving the bow and dip of her top lip a surreptitious lick?

Sleep. That was what he needed. A good night's sleep and he'd be seeing things more clearly.

"All right, then. What's this grand idea of yours?"

"Well!" She wove her hands together underneath her chin. "I know you're rehab royalty—"

"Along with a team of highly trained experts," Luca interrupted.

She didn't need to know he'd been dubbed the King

of Collagen before the accident had pushed him away from plastics to spinal injury rehabilitation. He probably would have carried on with plastics forever until—*bam!* In thirty horrifying seconds his life had changed.

He shook his head against the rising bile, forcing himself to focus on what Fran was saying.

"I read all of the bios for your clinicians last night, and there is some serious brainpower in play here." She dropped her hands. "Anyhow, I was thinking about the psychological advantages of being part of things here."

Luca gave her a sidelong look. "Do you mean you or the patients? All your chipping in has been much appreciated, Francesca. The painting, making the beds as promised... But if you read the résumés properly you will have noticed we have two very experienced psychiatrists on the team."

"I'm not talking about me and a paint roller. I'm thinking more hands-on stuff for the patients. There *is* the itty-bitty problem of half your village needing a splash more work done to it."

Her lips widened into an apologetic wince-smile.

"How very...political, Signorina Martinelli. I presume your plan includes *you* wrapping everything up nicely before your intended departure date?"

The smile dropped from Fran's face as quickly as the light fled from her eyes.

Luca could have kicked himself. Still shooting the messenger. Fran had been a trouper, working as hard as his paid staffers—if not harder—to get everything shipshape for the opening. She didn't deserve to be on the sharp end of his mood. Particularly seeing as he wasn't entirely sure he wasn't behaving like a boor in order to fight off the deepening attraction he felt to his resident sunflower.

"*Per favore*, Francesca." He forced himself to grind out the plea. "Please tell me your idea."

"Why, thank you very much!" She rubbed her hands together excitedly. "I can't really take credit for the idea, though. The other day I was watching online videos—you know, those feel-good ones where human spirit triumphs over adversity and you end up crying because people are so amazing?"

She looked across at the dubious expression he knew he was wearing and qualified her statement.

"The ones that make *me* cry anyway. So, there was this huge pile of bricks and a guy in a wheelchair—totally hot. Completely good-looking. Like you. But he was more…uh…*Nordic*."

She stopped, took a step back to consider him, and as their eyes caught a streak of pink blossomed on her cheeks.

"Let's not get carried away, here, Fran. Shall we?"

He gestured that they should continue along the stone-slab route they were making short work of. Fran scuttled ahead, rabbiting on about the video and only occasionally looking back at him. He was surprised to find he was smiling. At her unquenchable thirst for life? Or the fact she thought he was good-looking?

Foolish, really.

He shoved the thoughts away and forced himself to listen to her suggestion. It was the least he could do after his abrupt behavior.

By the time they reached the archway leading out to the bridge he'd been more than persuaded. Her idea was a good one.

"So what you're saying is if the patients—no matter what their background—put some actual graft into refurbishing the rest of the village, they'll be happier?"

"Precisely. I mean, this guy—totally paralyzed from the waist down—made just about the coolest fireplace out of bricks and mortar that I've ever seen. He *made* something. Crafted it with his own hands. Something many able-bodied people wouldn't even dream of starting, let alone finishing. I'm completely happy to oversee the project, of course. I know your team's hands are full."

She stood before him, blue eyes bright with expectation. Hope.

Tempting...

Pragmatics forced his hand.

"I hate to rain on your parade, Francesca, but there are thousands of other considerations. Health and safety, for one. You don't know how many inspections I have to deal with already—if I were to add patients to the mix of some already dangerous situations, I—"

He stopped himself. He'd been about to say he couldn't afford the insurance. Truth was he could hardly afford *any* of this. But turning it all over to the bank just so it could be demolished was out of the question. The clinic simply *had* to be a success.

"Look—" Fran raised her hands in a hear-me-out gesture "—I know what you're saying, and the idea definitely needs to be fleshed out. Especially as a lot of your patients are on the young side, right?"

"All of them." Luca nodded. "Teenagers."

"I'm not talking about everyone building stone walls or pizza ovens—although that *would* be a totally great idea. Can you imagine it? Pizza under the stars! What teenager doesn't love pizza?"

Luca glanced at his watch and spun his finger in a let's-get-on-with-it gesture, all the while trying his best not to get caught up in her enthusiasm.

His focus had to be X-ray machines. Crucial rehabilitation equipment being properly installed. Clipboards! If he'd known just how many clipboards he'd need when he'd started this pie-in-the-sky project...

"Sorry." She threw him an apologetic look. "I've just—I've just fallen a little bit in love with this place and it's hard to fight the enthusiasm, you know?"

Of course he knew. And her enthusiasm—despite his best efforts to be stoically distant—had touched his heart. His passion for the place was why he'd started the project in the first place. But now, with bills to pay and the bank breathing down his neck...

"I'm afraid it'll have to go on the pipe dreams list, Francesca."

Fran's disappointed expression soon brightened into something else. Inspiration.

"I've got an even better idea. I bet you there are any number of craftsmen who would love to come up here and work. True Italian craftsmen who wouldn't mind passing on some of their expertise to willing apprentices. Leather. Glass. Embossing. Calligraphy. I once saw an entire wall done in a painted leather wallpaper. It was amazing."

"We are *not* covering the walls in leather wallpaper, Fran."

"All right Mr. Grumpy. They don't have to be leather. Who cares what the patients do as long as they're happy? Even if it's just throwing a bit of paint on a wall. In the nicest way possible, of course," she finished with a polished smile.

"And what makes you think working on a building site will be an effective remedy for their ailments in comparison with the unparalleled medical attention they will be receiving here—*if* you ever let me get back to work, that is?"

Fran looked at him as if he was crazy.

"Who *doesn't* feel the satisfaction of a job well-done? Of knowing you've made an actual difference to somewhere this special. I mean, you must be *bursting* with pride."

A crackle of irritation flared in him.

"Francesca, the only thing I'm bursting with is the desire to untangle myself from this ridiculous conversation and get back to—"

Luca stopped in his tracks as they turned the corner of the archway into the main courtyard. Emotions ricocheted across his chest in hot thuds of recognition.

Humility. Pride. Achievement.

All the staff were assembled in the center of the broad arc—an impressive crowd of applauding doctors, rehab therapists, X-ray technicians and countless others. In the center was Pia and the two dogs. When her eyes lit on him she whispered a quick command to the dogs, each holding the end of a thick blue ribbon in their mouths, and they went in separate directions until it was taut and he could read the message on it. *"Bravo! I nostri migliori auguroni, Dr. Montovano!"*

The unfamiliar tickle of emotion teased at the back of Luca's throat.

Congratulations on a job well-done.

No one had done anything like this for him. *Ever.* His partners at the plastic surgery clinic had always mocked him for his pro bono cases. For bringing a bit of pride back into the life of a child with a birth defect or a scar that might have changed their lives forever. *Money!* they'd said. *The high life!*

He looked across at Fran. A flush of pleasure played across her cheeks as she watched him take it all in. The ridiculous conversation they'd been having made sense now. A distraction. Typical Fran. Perfection and mayhem in one maddening and beautiful package.

He felt torn. The sentiment of the moment was pure kindness.

"Zio! Come! Look at the food Fran has organized! It's all from artisan specialists in Tuscany!" Pia wheeled over to him and took his hand.

Behind the doctors and other medical practitioners—a team of about thirty, who were now reliant on him and the success of the clinic—were two trestle tables heaving under the weight of a bounty of antipasti, salads, savory tarts. All the regional specialties—and the people who had made them. Anything and everything a red-blooded Italian would crave if he were away from home.

He gruffly cleared his throat, giving them all a nod of thanks for their contributions.

More cries of *"Bravo!"* and *"Auguroni!"* filled the air.

He waved off the applause with a quick comment about how they were a team. How they all deserved a pat on the back for pulling together in the same way generations of villagers had back in the day when someone had been fool enough to start carving into the side of this blasted mountain and call it home.

Looking around at the smiling faces, hearing the laughter, feeling the buzz of anticipation in the air, he allowed himself a brief moment of elation. If he could hold on to that feeling—

Luca's eyes lit upon Fran, the only woman in the world who would have bothered to make this moment happen.

Something deep within him twisted and ached. Longed to have a spare ounce of energy, an unfettered moment to explore…test the waters and see what would happen if he and Fran were to—

Enough.

He couldn't even hold on to a girlfriend he'd no plans to marry, let alone pay enough attention to his niece.

Pia and the clinic. His two priorities. Everything else—everyone else—would have to wait.

Fran saw the lift in Luca's eyes as he scanned the team. The glint of renewed energy. The gratifying blaze of pride. She hoped he knew just how proud all of these people were of *him*. Of the life he'd brought not only to Mont di Mare but to the community as a whole. A center of excellence, right here in their own little hideaway nook of Italy!

"Cut the ribbon!"

The call originated from Pia, but soon everyone was chanting it.

A nurse ran up to Luca with a small pair of surgical scissors from her hip kit when Pia put out a panicked call that she'd remembered the ribbon but not the scissors. The dogs were instructed to stand at either side of the archway in front of Luca, and as the scissors swept through the silken sash, marking this historic moment, Luca's eyes met Fran's.

It was impossible to read his expression, but the effect his gaze had upon her body was hard to deny. The explosion of internal fireworks. Her bloodstream soaring in temperature. The roar in her ears while the rest of her body filled with a showering cascade of never-ending sparks. The feeling that she was less mortal than she had been before.

She gave herself a sharp shake.

She was here to do a job. Not to get all doe-eyed over the boss man. And yet…was that a hint of softness in Luca's gaze? A concession that she might *not* be the thorn in his side he'd initially pegged her to be.

Little sparkles of pleasure swirled around her belly at the thought. Sparkles she was going to have to round up and tame if doing her job and leaving this place with her heart intact were her intentions.

She felt a set of familiar fingers giving her hand a tug.

Pia. Her golden-hearted charge. The entire point of her being there.

"What do you say we get some food?" Fran asked.

"Sounds good to me." Pia swirled her chair around then looked up at her. "Fran?"

"Mmm-hmm?" Fran pulled her attention back from another surreptitious glance in Luca's direction.

"You're good for him, you know."

"Beg pardon?" Fran's attention was fully on Pia now.

"Uncle Luca. He's a bit like me, I think."

Fran swallowed a disbelieving laugh out of respect for Pia's serious tone. "In what way?"

Pia's expression turned suddenly shy, and her fingers teased at the belt that held her petite torso in place against the low back of her chair.

"He's a bit lonely, I think. He works so hard. And with all the pressure my...my condition must put on him I can't help but worry that he's going to work himself to death. I know he loves medicine and everything, but what if this is all too much for him? What if...?" Pia's voice broke, though she maintained eye contact and tried again. "What if...?"

Fran's heart felt as though it were going to burst with compassion when Pia's eyes filled with tears. The amount of loss the poor girl had endured and now she feared losing her uncle, as well? She saw that Luca was trying to spend time with Pia, but she also knew the long hours he put in with the clinic. It was exactly what had happened with her father and his cars. Even when he was at home he wasn't really there. And getting access to his heart was near impossible.

Fran pulled Pia's hands into hers and gave each set of the girl's knuckles a quick kiss. "Don't you worry, *amore*. As long as I'm here we'll make sure your uncle is looked after."

No matter how hard a task it was.

They both looked across to where Luca was standing. He'd stepped away from the crowd now, and a smattering of antipasti was near enough tipping off the plate he barely seemed to notice he was holding.

The team of doctors and support staff had all formed groups, or were crowding around the table, piling delicacies onto their own plates. Luca's body was drawn up to his full height. Six feet of *leave me alone*. His attention was utterly unwavering as he gazed upon the clinic's entryway. His expression was hooded, once again, heavy with the burden of all that had yet to be done.

CHAPTER SEVEN

LUCA SAW THE helicopter before he heard it. A tiny speck heading in from Florence—the whirring blades, the long body of a medical helicopter with its telltale red cross on the undercarriage coming into view as it crested the "hills," as Francesca insisted upon calling them.

As if his thinking her name had conjured her up, she appeared by his side. "Are you excited?"

"Focused. I have my first surgery today. Shouldn't you be working with Pia? Where are the dogs?"

Fran gave him a sidelong look, clearly unimpressed by his curt tone. "They're with her algebra tutor. Pia wanted me to give you this." She handed him an envelope, but not before shooting him a ha!-take-that look. "She wanted to wish you luck," she continued. "As do I."

Luca pushed the card into his pocket, returning his gaze to the approaching helicopter.

This is work. Fran is...pleasure. There's no room for pleasure in my life.

Despite himself, he turned and watched Fran as she tracked the arrival of the *elicottero*, her chin tipped up toward the sky, the movement elongating the length of her slender neck, the fine outline of her face, the sweet spot where her neck met her jaw. If he were to kiss her there would she groan or whimper with pleasure? Would her legs slip up and around his waist, tugging him in deeper, more fully into her, so that with each thrust he took—

"Dr. Montovano?"

"*Si*, Elisa?" He stopped and corrected himself. "Dr. Sovani. What can I do for you?"

Luca forced his attention to narrow and focus as the doctor rattled through the plans for their patient's arrival and presurgical procedures. He didn't miss Fran's fingers sweeping up to cover the twist of her lips—a snigger at his obviously divided attentions.

She'd obviously caught him staring. Seen the desire in his eyes.

Something in him snapped. Didn't she *know* how vital today was for him and the clinic? The bank had already been on the phone that morning to remind him. *Tick-tock.*

"Miss Martinelli, do you mind? We've got a surgery to prepare for."

She didn't say a word. Didn't have to. Disdain for his dismissive tone was written all over her face.

"Did you want Paolo to go up to the main buildings first, or to his quarters?" Dr. Sovani asked.

"We should get him straight to a prep room." Luca blinkered his vision, forced himself to train his eyes on Elisa's clipboard. "He'll be tired after his journey, and his family would no doubt like to see him settled. The operation isn't for a couple of hours, and we'll need him at his strongest. Are his parents in the chopper with him?"

"They're arriving by car."

As if on cue, a couple appeared in the archway leading to the helicopter landing area, two young children alongside them, all eyes trained on the sky as their loved one approached.

The instant the helicopter touched down, the air was filled with rapid-fire instructions, questions and action.

Fran was nowhere to be seen.

"*Ciao*, Paolo." Luca strode to the teenager's side once the heli-medics had lifted him into his wheelchair and ensured the helmet protecting his skull was in place. "What do you say we head to the clinic and get you settled?"

If Pia hadn't asked, Fran wouldn't have dreamed of stepping foot anywhere near the clinic. But she'd pleaded with Fran to let her take a break from her studies and watch her uncle in surgery. Now that they were here, in the observation room, she had to admit it was amazing.

"Can you turn the speaker up, please, Francesca?" Pia's fingers were covering her mouth, and her body was taut, as if she were watching a blockbuster movie, not a surgery meant to restore a portion of a patient's skull.

"Do you know what happened to him?" Fran asked.

"I don't know the whole story, but he was in a *moto* accident, I think. A year ago. They had to take out part of his skull because of the swelling. The surgeons in Florence said Zio Luca would be the best person to replace it, so they've waited until now. The last thing he needed was a terrible surgeon *and* to be left with a dent in his head!"

Fran smiled at the pride in Pia's voice. Of *course* she was proud. Her surgeon uncle was finally doing what he loved best. Fran could see that now. Sure, he had held his own with a hammer, and seemed to have no problem understanding complicated spreadsheets—but this... Seeing him here in the operating theater was mesmerizing.

The assured sound of his voice as he spoke to the nurses turned her knees to putty, and the exacting movement of his hands was both delicate and confident. It was little wonder he'd seemed like a pent-up ball of frustration in the week leading up to the clinic's opening. He hadn't been doing what he obviously did best: medicine.

"Francesca?" Pia was tapping a finger on her hand.

"Yes—sorry. What is it, *amore*?"

Pia giggled, then singsonged, "Someone's got a crush on Zio Luca!"

"I do *not*!" Fran protested. A bit too hotly, maybe. Just a little. But in a never-ever-going-to-happen kind of way. A flight of fancy.

"Just as well." Pia returned her gaze to the OR window as if she saw that sort of thing all the time. "He's a terrible boyfriend. Too bad you're the only girlfriend I like."

"And you can carry on liking me. Just not as your uncle's girlfriend."

"Maybe not *now*..." Pia teased, her eyes still glued to her uncle.

Maybe not *ever*, Fran told herself, refusing to let the seeds of imagination take root. It was far too easy to imagine those hands touching her body. His full lips, now hidden behind a surgical mask, touching and tasting her own...

She froze when she realized Luca was looking at her. His eyebrows cinched together in confusion. He obviously hadn't been aware he had an audience. Then they lifted, and little crinkles appeared at the corners of his eyes as if he were smiling behind his mask.

A whirl of something heated took a tour around her chest and swirled lazily in her stomach.

All she could think of to do was to point at Pia, then give him a double thumbs-up and a cheesy grin as if he'd just managed to flip a pancake, not perform an incredibly intricate reconstructive surgery.

What an idiot!

If she'd stood even the tiniest chance of being Luca's girlfriend a second ago—not that she *wanted* to be his girlfriend—she'd definitely closed the door of opportunity right down. Luca only took people seriously if *they* were serious. Whether he thought she was cute or not was beside the point. She wanted him to take her as seriously as she took him.

Pia and the dogs. She needed to repeat it like a mantra. *Pia and the dogs.* They were her only focus. Not the other patients. Not the beautiful village. Not the tall, dark and enigmatically talented surgeon putting the final stitches into his first surgery at his new clinic.

He was a picture of utter concentration.

There wasn't room for her in his life.

Never had been.

Never would be.

The best thing she could do now was focus on getting Pia up to speed, then going home and mending fences with her father. He was the only man she should be worrying about impressing.

CHAPTER EIGHT

A SURGE OF pride filled Luca's heart on seeing the new ramps and pathways being put to use as they'd been intended.

Just a few days in and Mont di Mare felt *alive*. More dynamic than it had in years.

His sister would be so proud of what they'd done with the place. If only bank loans could be repaid with good feelings...

Never mind. Treatments were underway. However slowly, payments were starting to come in to counterbalance the flood of outgoing costs.

The surgery with Paolo had gone as smoothly as he'd hoped. The teenager was already out of Recovery, and at this very moment discussing the litany of tests he would be going through to combat further deterioration in the wake of his paralysis.

Luca itched to join Paolo's team, to be part of adding more movement to the young man's upper body after his motor scooter accident had paralyzed him from the waist down. It was a similar injury to his niece's, only he'd received next to no physio in the wake of his accident.

The lack of strength in his upper body was startling. Just thinking about the various avenues of treatment they could explore made him smile.

"Dr. Montovano?" Elisa appeared at the doorway. "We've got Giuliana, ready to discuss her case with you."

"Great! Is she in her room?"

"No, she's over by the pool, speaking with your... your friend?"

Luca's brow cinched. "Friend?"

"You know—the one with the dogs."

"Ah. Francesca. No, she's not a friend. She's here to work with Pia."

The words hit false notes even as they came out. A familiar feeling began to take hold of him. The feeling that he'd started to let someone in and then, slowly but surely, had begun to push her away again. Just as he'd done with Marina. Just as he'd done with the women before her.

Elisa shifted uncomfortably, a soft blush coloring her cheeks. "Apologies... We weren't sure..."

"We?" Luca's alarm bells started ringing.

"The team. We didn't—she just..." Elisa's eyes scanned his office in a panic. "She seems to do a lot more than someone who is just here with the assistance dogs would."

"Yes, she's very...*American*," he said, as if it explained everything.

Elisa nodded, clearly none the wiser.

"Va bene," he said, in a tone he knew suggested otherwise. "Shall we go and have a chat with Giuliana?"

"It's all right. You can pet him if you like." Fran smiled at the teen, well aware that Giuliana's fingers had been twitching on her wheelchair arm supports ever since she and Edison had appeared in the courtyard adjacent to the infinity pool.

The pool she was absolutely dying to jump into now that summer had well and truly made an appearance.

When Giuliana's parents had mistaken her for medical staff and asked if she would look after their daughter while they went to see her room, she had said yes.

Foolish? Perhaps.

But everyone was operating at full capacity now that the clinic was open, and with Pia already busy with her studies what harm could a little babysitting do?

The dark-haired girl looked across at her with a despondent look. "It's my arms. They're just so weak."

"You've got to start somewhere," Fran reminded her gently. "Not to mention the fact you're in the perfect place to start rebuilding that strength."

Fran tried to shake away the problem with a smile, hiding an internal sympathy twinge. Giuliana's arms were strapped to stabilizing arm troughs and wrist supports on her chair. They were so thin it was almost frightening.

"Edison." Fran issued a couple of commands and the Lab bounded over and sat alongside Giuliana, so that his head was directly in line with the armrest. "Is it all right if I undo your strap?"

A hint of anxiety crossed the girl's eyes. "Are my parents back yet?"

Fran looked around, vividly aware of how restricted the poor girl's movement was. Her neck was being cradled by two contoured pads and it didn't seem as if she had the strength—let alone the capacity—to turn it left or right.

"They don't seem to be. They were going to look at your room, right?"

"Si..." Giuliana replied glumly. "They have to approve every single little thing before I am even allowed to see it. I can hardly believe they left me alone with *you.*"

Tough for any teen to have helicopter parents. Even harder when there was zero choice in the matter.

Fran bit her cheek when Giuliana gave the telltale eye roll of an exasperated teen. She didn't know how many times *she'd* rolled her eyes behind her dad's back when he'd made yet another unilateral decision on her behalf.

Her hand slipped to her back pocket to check her phone was still there. They hadn't talked yet today.

Time zones.

She'd call him later. Just knowing he'd pick up the phone now, close his laptop and really talk to her, made such a difference. Giuliana might find her parents annoying, but at least they were *there* for her.

"It doesn't really hurt when my hands are out of the supports…" Giuliana was saying.

"Do you mind me asking what happened?"

"Skiing." The word sounded as lifeless as the faraway look in Giuliana's eyes.

"Where was the injury?" Fran asked.

When she'd been a physio being straightforward with her questions had usually paid dividends. No need to tip-toe around patients who were facing a life of paralysis.

"Grade-four whiplash. Cervical spine fracture."

"C1?" Francesca asked, her jaw dropping. Most people would have died.

"C2."

"Oof! That must've hurt." Fran's features widened into a "youch" face. She was still lucky. C2 fractures often resulted in fatalities.

"Quite the opposite," Giuliana answered drily. "I didn't feel a thing."

"Ha! Of course you didn't!"

Fran hooted with laughter before registering the look of disbelief on Giuliana's face. *Oops.*

"I'm sorry, *amore*. You'll have to forgive me. I'm used

to talking to dogs, not humans. I am a class-A expert in Open Mouth, Insert Foot."

Giuliana considered her for a moment, then gave a wry smile. "Actually, it was my test. You just passed."

"Oh!" Fran gave a little wriggle of pride that morphed into a hunch of concern. "Wait a minute. What kind of test?"

"A test to see who will laugh at the poor crippled girl's joke."

"A joke test?"

"A litmus test," Giuliana answered solidly. "Most people don't even ask me what happened. They just look at me with big sad eyes, like I'm on the brink of death or something. I'm paralyzed. Not deaf or blind!"

And not bereft of spirit either, from the looks of things.

Fran let loose an appreciative whoop of respect. "You go, girl!" She put her hand up in a fist bump, rolled her eyes at her second idiotic move within as many minutes, then put her fist to Giuliana's anyway. "Forgive me. *Again.* You're here for the summer?"

Giuliana nodded, amusement skittering through her eyes.

"Well, I don't know what your doctor's plans are, but by the end of our stay what do you say we work toward a proper fist bump?"

"What? So you can be 'down with the kids'?" Giuliana giggled, as if the idea of Francesca being down with the kids was quite the challenge.

"Yeah!" Fran parried, striking a silly pose. "That's how I roll. Hey! I have an idea." She positioned herself so she was at eye level with Giuliana. "How crazy are you feeling today?"

"In what way?"

The teen's brow crinkled and it was all Fran could do

not to reach out and give it a soothing caress. She couldn't promise the girl that everything would be all right, and nor did she have the right to do anything other than what Luca had hired her to do, but…

"Well, Edison here is my number one gentle dog…"

It wasn't a lie. Not really. Her *other* number one dog was already completely under Pia's command.

"If you'd like to pet him, it seems to me the easiest way to do it would be if we unstrapped you. I would be right behind you, supporting your elbow, and Edison is very good at holding his head still."

The glimmer of excitement in Giuliana's eyes was all the encouragement Fran needed. Ever so gently, Fran lifted the girl's frail arm out of the rest and settled it in her lap for a moment.

"Is it all right if I put a treat in your hand?" Fran asked. "It's a sure-fire way to get Edison's full attention."

"I don't know how well I'll be able to hold it."

"Not a problem. I'll support you."

Fran pinched a treat out of her belt pouch, placed it between Giuliana's fragile fingers with Edison sitting at full attention at her feet. Then Fran shifted around behind the wheelchair, so she could provide support for the girl's elbow. It surprised her to feel how rigid the poor thing's arm was—similar to some of the elderly people she'd worked with years ago. Something deep within her bridled. How awful to have to live like this with your whole life in front of you!

Don't get attached, Fran! You gave up on people for a reason. First, fix things with your father…

Her thoughts faded as instinctively she began to massage the girl's arm. Stroking and smoothing her fingers along the length of the musculature, teasing some suppleness into the brittle length of her arm.

"Come, Edison. Want a treat?"

Giuliana's hand jerked as she spoke. The treat went flying. As it arced up so, too, did Edison's snout, his jaw opening wide as he jumped up to catch it.

"What the *hell* do you think you're doing?"

Luca was thundering across the patio, his face dark as midnight.

By the time he arrived Edison was contentedly swallowing the treat he'd caught, with no detriment to Giuliana whatsoever.

"We were just—" Fran began, then she stopped as memory swept her back to her sixteenth birthday. The one her father had forgotten because it had been the same day his first car had rolled off the production line.

All day she had stayed at the factory. Doing home-work…idly peeking into the kitchen at the canteen to see if anyone was secretly whipping up a birthday cake. Wandering through the advertising section on the off chance that someone had made a little—or an enormous—birthday banner to mark the day. Hanging around in the mailroom on the pretense of helping to sort the large bundle of post, only to discover that her mother had, as usual, neglected to send anything.

When at long last the first car had come off the assembly line—that first amazing vehicle—she had been so excited she'd run up to touch it, to press her face to the window. The second her hand had touched the car her father had seized her wrist and pulled her away so hard it had hurt for a week.

He hadn't meant to hurt her. She knew that. But it was in that instant that she'd forced herself to take her first significant emotional step away from him.

That same week she had been signed up for her first round of finishing school in Switzerland. And then another and another, until the thick wedge of her self-protection had been permanently driven between them.

The flash of ire lighting up Luca's eyes was near enough identical to the one she'd seen in her father's eyes when she'd dared lay her hand on something that wasn't hers.

In Luca's eyes she'd just crossed the line.

His patient. His clinic. His future.

Her mistake.

"Dr. Montovano! Did you *see* that?"

Luca could just hear Giuliana's voice through the static roaring in his ears. He was still reeling at how careless Fran was. *Reckless!*

"*Scusi*, Giuliana. See what?" Luca forced himself to turn to his new patient, hastily removing from his eyes the daggers he'd been shooting at Fran.

This was a clinic for people with *spinal injuries*, for heaven's sake. Had she no respect for what he was trying to do here? No understanding that the slightest mishap could shut him down?

"The dog!" Giuliana said, the smile so broad across her face he hardly recognized her as the same girl captured in the glowering, unhappy photos her parents had sent. "Did you see how when I threw the treat he caught it?"

"He was catching a treat?"

"*Si, Dottore.* Of course. What did you think he was doing?"

Fran turned to him, arms crossed defensively across her chest, with a look that said, *I'd certainly like to know what it was you thought Edison was doing.*

The dog had been jumping, its mouth wide-open, teeth bared. It had looked as if it had been launching himself at

the girl's hand. Which—on went a lightbulb—of *course*
he had. She had been throwing a treat.

Another lightbulb joined the first.

"I thought you didn't have any movement in your
arm."

"I didn't…" Giuliana replied, her expression changing as she, too, began connecting the dots of an enormous puzzle.

"Mind if I have a quick feel?" Luca knelt, and with his
young patient's consent he took her arm in his hands and
began to run his fingers along the different muscle and
ligament groups in her forearm. Her fingers responded to
a few of his manipulations. Fingers that were, according
to her physio at home, completely atrophied from disuse.

"Shall we get you into one of the treatment rooms?
See what may have happened there?"

"*Si.* Can Edison come, too? And Francesca? She massaged my arm before I fed Edison."

A flash of ire blinded him again for an instant.

Why couldn't Fran keep to herself?

He hesitated for a moment before looking up, forcing
himself to take a slow breath. She was a trained physio.
This was meant to be a place of innovation. And now
that he was repainting the scene into what it had actually been, it was very likely Fran and Edison had each
played a role in eliciting movement in Giuliana's arm.

By the time he lifted his eyes to offer an invitation
he saw that none was necessary. Fran and Edison were
disappearing through an archway leading to the wildflower meadows.

A sour twist of enmity tightened around his heart. He
didn't need to push Fran away. She had already gone.

CHAPTER NINE

A KNOCK SOUNDED on the door frame of Fran's cottage. It was so unexpected she nearly jumped out of her skin. And she was half-naked. More than half-naked, really.

The baby-doll nightgown had been a spontaneous, lacy gift to herself when she'd gone bridesmaid-dress shopping with Bea. A nod to the femininity she knew lurked somewhere inside her but that she'd never quite had the courage to explore.

"*Scusi*, Francesca, do you have a moment?"

Little frissons of awareness tickled up along her neck when she heard Luca's voice. Sprays of goose bumps followed in their wake when she turned the corner and saw him. One hand flew to cover her chest and the other stupidly groped for and tugged at the bottom-skimming hemline.

"Yes, of course. What can I help you with?"

"I think I owe you an apology."

"Ah, well…"

Please quit staring at my half-naked body.

"No need. I understand—"

"No. I was too sharp. The truth is…" Luca paused and looked up toward the stars just beginning to shine out against the night sky.

The truth is what? An icy chill spread through her. Was he going to send her away?

She nodded, tugging at the spaghetti straps of her nightdress as if the soupçon of flesh they covered would disguise the fact that the plunging neckline and tiny triangles of lace barely covering her breasts were advertising the fact she hadn't had sex in… Oh…who was counting anyway? Celibacy was the "in" thing, right? Or did the nightdress say the opposite? That she was a floozy and had been hanging out with her front door open just waiting for him to—

Stop. Just stop. Act normal. Relaxed. As if gorgeous Italian doctors who can't bear the sight of you are always popping by for a casual you're-fired chat.

"I think I know why you're here." Fran decided to fill the growing silence. "Making sure we continue in the same vein as we started, right? Frenemies forever!"

Luca's brows hitched closer together.

"Frenemies?" She tried again. "Friends who are enemies?"

He shook his head.

She shifted her shoulder straps again, trying to feel less naked.

This whole standing-here-in-silence thing was getting a little annoying. She had dignity. Brains. Self-esteem.

C'mon, Frannie. Pull it together.

"Luca, is there anything I can help you with? Some last-minute painting…?"

Still too chirpy. Dial back the cheerleader… Bring in the helpful canine-assistance trainer.

Tough when Luca was just standing there staring at her, refusing to engage in her inane one-sided conversation.

"I was not thinking frenemies. I was thinking employee."

"What?" *Unexpected.* "You want me to *work* for you?"

He nodded—yes.

"One of my physios has returned to Rome. The rural location didn't seem to suit him."

"Is he nuts?" Fran was shocked. "I mean Rome is great, but this place is just about as close to heaven as it gets! I'd stay here forever if I could. I mean, not *forever*, forever…just…"

"Francesca. *Per favore*, will you just answer the question?"

"Of course. I'll do anything to help." She held up a finger. "On one condition."

A crease of worry deepened the scar on his cheek—the one she was dying to ask about but already had a pretty good guess had something to do with his orphaned niece being in a car accident. They all added up to a picture no one would keep in their wallet.

But now wasn't the time.

"Luca, listen. I would love to do the work—but only if you let me do it gratis."

"Oh, no—"

Francesca held up a hand to protest.

"Don't take it the wrong way. This would be helping *me*."

Luca laughed, but not because he thought she was funny. "I hardly think not paying you is *helping*."

"It would." She reached out to the side table and wiggled her phone between them. "See…my dad and I have been having daily talks in advance of my return. I've been trying to convince him for years to let me do charitable work in the name of his company. If you'd let me work on the patients and make little video diaries of their

progress as I went—with their permission, of course—
I think it might be a way to persuade him to let me do
more of the same when I get home."

"I thought you were through with treating people?"

She shrugged. "Some people are worth changing your
mind for."

The words hit their mark. Luca's dark eyes sought her
own and when their gazes caught and cinched tight she
could hardly breathe. She'd meant *patients*. But from all
the tiny hairs standing up on her arms, something was
telling her there had just been a shift between them.

As suddenly as the air had gone taut between them
it relaxed. As if Luca had sought and found the answer
to the questions racing through his eyes. She sucked in
a breath of mountain air, her heart splitting wide-open.
More than she'd allowed for anyone else.

He looked tired, his hair all helter-skelter, as if he'd
been repeatedly running a worried hand through it.
Though he wore smart attire, he still had on paint-stained,
sawdust-covered work boots.

Her eyes were trained on his boots because she wasn't
brave enough to look up into those dark eyes of his again.
And then she dared.

A flush of heat struck her cheeks like a slap when she
realized the flash of emotion she'd seen in his eyes was
the same one alight in hers.

Desire.

"I also wanted a quick word about Pia…" Luca began.

"Pia! Yes. Good. All's going blue blazes in *that* camp."
She tried to strike a casual pose. Tricky when she was
half-naked in front of a man whose mere presence made
her nipples tighten. "I think Freda's the dog for her. Those
two seem inseparable."

"Is that a good thing? Being so close?" Luca uncrossed his arms. "What about boundaries?"

Was he still talking about Pia and her dog?

"Well, boundaries are gray areas."

Luca's eyebrow arched. "Oh?"

"But they need to be clear. Boundaries definitely need to be very, very clear."

"Clear enough so that each party knows exactly what they're getting into?"

Luca reached up and rested a crooked arm along the wooden beam above her door frame. Where had stern-faced, humorless Luca gone? There wasn't time to think. Sexy Luca's sun-heated man scent was invading her senses, whooshing through her like a drug.

He definitely wasn't talking about the dogs anymore.

Just as well. There was no room for any thought in her head other than the knowledge that she wanted him. She wanted to jump into his arms, wrap her legs around his trim waist and kiss the living daylights out of him. Touch his scar. Get stubble burn. Ache between her legs from hours of lovemaking. *Hell!* She'd dance around on tiptoe for the next three weeks if he would just scoop her up and have his wicked way with her.

"How does one *establish* these boundaries?" Luca asked, the tension between them thickening with each passing moment.

Gone was the uptight, form-filling timekeeper. In his place was a sensualist. His shoulders shifted, roll-ing beneath the thick cotton of his shirt with the grace of a mountain lion, and his eyes were alight with need. With hunger.

Heat tickled and teased across Fran's skin, swirling and pooling between her legs.

Per amor del cielo!

Luca let the door frame take some of his weight, bringing him even closer to her.

There was no disguising her body's response to him. Goose bumps shot up her arms. Her breasts were taut, arching toward him as if they had a will of their own.

Did she really want this? Him? Maybe he was right. Clear-cut boundaries were exactly what they needed if either of them was to survive the summer. Then again, sex was an excellent way to cut tension...

No. They needed to talk this out. Like grown-ups. With clothes on.

"Did you want to...um...?"

She pointed toward the bedroom, where her bathrobe was hanging. It was a scrubby terry-cloth number covered in images of Great Danes wearing nerdy spectacles. Her gaze returned to Luca's. As the hit of electricity that only seemed to grow each time their eyes met took effect she lost the power of speech. She'd meant "should she go get her robe and so they could sit down for a talk and a coffee." Or a nightcap. Not "should they go for a roll in the hay"!

Before Fran's brain could comprehend what was happening Luca had pulled her into his arms and was lowering his mouth to hers with a heated passion she had never felt before. There was an urgency in his kisses. A thrilling assurance in his touch. As if they were long-lost lovers separated by oceans, reunited by their unquenchable thirst for each other.

The ardor pouring from his body to hers began to flow between them in an ever-growing circle—floodwaters unleashed. There was nothing chaste about their kisses. They were needy, insatiable. Words escaped her as he tasted and explored first her lips and then her mouth with every bit as much passion as she put into touching and experiencing him. The occasional brush of stubble. The burr of a growl as she nibbled and then softly bit his lower lip before opening her mouth as he teased her lips apart with his tongue.

A soft groan escaped Fran's already kiss-bruised lips as one of Luca's hands slid to the small of her back and tugged her in tight to him; the other slipped around to the nape of her neck. She felt his fingers weave through the length of her hair, then tug it back so that her neck lay bare to him. It wasn't cruelty or domination. It was unfettered desire. The same ache rendering her both powerless and energized in his arms.

Willing away the millions of thoughts that might have shut the moment down, Fran closed her eyes and allowed the sensations of Luca's touch to spread through her veins. With the pad of his thumb he tipped her head to the side. His lips pulled away from hers. Before she had a chance to experience any loss she could feel their heated presence again, tasting and kissing the sensitive nook between her chin and neck.

His fingers moved from the back of her head to the other side of her neck, his thumb drawing along the length of her throat as his lips did the same on the exposed length of her neck. She could feel the pads of his fingers tracing from her shoulder to her collarbone, dipping down to the swell of her breasts. She couldn't help it. She arched into his hands, her body longing for more.

Unexpectedly, Luca cupped her face in both his hands and tipped his forehead to hers, his breath coming as swiftly as her heartbeat, which was racing to catch up with what was happening.

"*Scusi*, Francesca. I'm so sorry."

She heard the words but his body told a different story as his hands tugged her ever so slightly closer toward him. Her hands rose to his chest and confirmed what she'd suspected. His heart was racing as quickly as her own.

"I'm not…" she managed to whisper.

"This isn't why I came here."

"Stay." The word was out before she could stop it.

"I have nothing to offer you." Luca's voice was raw, as if the words had scraped past his throat against his will.

"I don't remember asking for anything," Fran said, her feet arching up onto tiptoe, her lips grazing his as she spoke.

"I need boundaries."

"So do I."

Fran meant the words with all her heart. She felt as if her whole body was on fire, and without protecting her heart she'd never survive the summer.

Luca held her out at arm's length, examining her face as if his life depended upon it.

"What did you say we were?"

Fran ran their conversation through her head at lightning speed, then laughed. "Frenemies?"

Luca nodded. "Will that do?"

"Colleagues by day, lovers by night?" she countered.

He nodded his assent. "No more talking."

Their lips met again, to explosive effect. In just those few moments his touch had already changed. Where there had been tentative exploration now there was fire behind his kisses. Intimacy. As if each erotically charged touch was laying claim to her, physically altering the chemical makeup of her bloodstream. What had once felt heavy now became light. Effervescent, even. In each other's arms they were no longer bound to the earth. They were in orbit—two celestial bodies exploring, teasing, coaxing, arousing.

Fran's breasts were swollen with longing, her nipples taut against the sheer lace of her nightgown. As Luca's hand swept across her bottom his fingers just grazed the sensitive pulsing between her legs, forcing her to bite back a cry of pleasure. He drew his fingers up and along her spine, rendering her core completely molten. She'd experienced lust in the past, but now she became vividly aware that she had never known desire. Not like this. She'd never craved a man's touch as much as she yearned for Luca's.

"Mio piccola passerotta..."

Fran felt Luca's breath glide along her neck as he whispered into her ear. *His little sparrow.* If anyone in the world could make her feel like a delicate bird in flight…

Don't think. Just be.

Abruptly she tugged her fingers down the back of his neck, the pressure of her nails eliciting a groan of pleasure as once again he tipped her head back and dropped kisses along the length of her neck, his fingers tracing the delicate dips and swells of her décolletage.

Fran inhaled deeply—everything about this moment would form the scent palate she would return to when the day came she had to leave. Late-night jasmine. Pepper. Wood shavings. The sun-warmed heat of early summer and tanned skin.

She tipped her head forward as Luca's hands slid along her sides and pulled her close to his chest. Another scent she'd remember forever. One very particular chest, attached to the most intriguing man she had ever laid eyes on.

A particle of insecurity lodged itself in her heart as she became aware of his hands sweeping along the curve of her shoulders to her arms. It took a second to connect mind and body. He was holding her out—away from him—so that he could tip her chin up and their eyes would meet.

And when they did it was like a lightning strike.

One so powerful she knew what she was feeling was more than chemical.

"You must want something. Everyone does."

Respect. Love. Of course she wanted love. Marriage. Family. The whole nine yards one day. But Luca was the worst person in the world to start *that* sort of craziness with. And the last.

"We couldn't have met at a worse time," he continued.

"Or in a less promising way," she reminded him, unable to keep that moment at the basilica from popping into her mind. "You and I will never be friends."

Oh, the irony! And look at them now, woven into one another's arms as if their being together had been predestined.

And that was when it hit her. What it was she wanted from a relationship.

To be lit up from within as she had been these last few precious moments. To feel elemental. Woven into the very fabric of someone else's being.

She lowered her eyelids to half-mast. Luca didn't need access to the tempest flaring between her heart and mind.

Her heart was near enough thumping out of her chest. She'd never done anything this...*intentional* before. Offering herself to him only to zip up what was left of her heart and take it away at the end of the summer.

She looked at Luca, all super masculine and reserved. Every bit the courtly gent by day, but by night a wild boy up for a bit of rough and tumble, if his kisses were anything to go by. His five-o'clock shadow was thick with the late hour, cheekbones taut, lips bloodred from their kisses. The scar she was longing not only to trace with her finger but her tongue...

"Let's do it." She moved her hand into the thin wedge of space between them. "Frenemies. Boundary hunters. Whatever you like. Shake on it?"

Luca didn't want to shake hands. He wanted to take possession of her. Become intimately acquainted with every particle of Francesca he could get his hands on. He wanted to touch and caress all that he could see and all that he couldn't beneath the tiny bits of fabric that made up her excuse for a nightgown. To disappear in her beauty and reemerge fortified and vital. Ready to take on anyone and anything.

Fran's hand pressed against his chest as he pulled her tight to him so she could feel the effect she had on him. Her eyes widened and a distinctly saucy laugh burbled up from her throat. She wanted him as much as he wanted her. He could see it in her eyes, feel it in the tipped points of her nipples as they abraded his chest when she wriggled in his arms.

"I've got something better than a handshake in mind for you," he murmured.

"Oh, *do* you now?"

Fran's feline eyes were sultry. She tipped her chin toward him with a smile edging onto the corners of her lips. A naughty smile.

Dio! She was beautiful.

In one swift move he kicked the door shut with his booted foot, swept her up into his arms and carried her without further ceremony straight to her bedroom.

She whooped when he all but tossed her onto the mattress, showing scant restraint as he stretched out alongside her. He was clearly enjoying the soft groan of pleasure he elicited when he ran a hand over the tips of her breasts before brusquely pushing aside the tiny triangles of lace and lowering his lips onto first one, then the other taut nipple, his tongue circling the deep pink of her areolae as he leisurely slid his hand across her belly and down to rest between her legs.

Luca's breath caught, his lips just barely touching her nipple, as Fran pressed against his fingers. She grabbed for his free hand, drawing each of his fingers, one at a time, into her mouth, giving each one a wicked swirl of the tongue, a teasing lick and a suck.

Forcing himself to ignore the growing intensity building below his waistline, Luca slid his fingers beneath the thin strip at the base of Fran's panties, delighting in the heated dew of her response to his touch. He had become utterly consumed with bringing her pleasure.

So responsive to his touch was she, he had to check himself again and again not to move too rapidly. To draw out her pleasure for as long as he could. When at last her body grew taut with expectation and desire, he unleashed his hands from their earlier restraint, let his mouth explore the most tender nooks of her belly, licking and teasing at the very tip of her most sensitive area until she cried out with pleasure and release.

Fran grabbed the sides of his face and roughly pulled his mouth toward hers. "Naked. Now!" were the only two words he could make out between her cries of pleasure as he dipped his fingers in farther, teasing and tempting her to reach another climax.

"Protection?"

An impressive stream of Italian gutter talk flowed as Fran lurched out of the bed, ran to the bathroom, clattered through who knew what at a high rate of knots and reappeared in the doorway, framed by the soft light of the bathroom, with a triumphant smile on her face and a small packet held between two fingers.

"Bridesmaid favors! Now, take off your clothes," Fran commanded, already taking deliberate steps toward the bed. *"Now."*

A broad smile peeled his lips apart. This made a nice change from the needy women he tended to attract. The ones who wanted the title, the property, but not the work that came along with the mantle he'd been forced to wear.

"Is this how it's going to work?" Luca asked, propping himself up on an elbow as he watched her approach like a lioness about to pounce for the kill. "You giving me orders?"

"Tonight it is." Fran straddled him in one fluid move, the bold glint in her eyes hinting at pleasures yet to unfold.

He needed this. He needed *her*.

"Well, then…" Luca arched an eyebrow at her and began unbuttoning his shirt. "I suppose it would be foolish not to oblige."

Fran batted his hands away and ripped off the rest of the buttons of his shirt, her hands swirling possessively across the expanse of his chest.

"Yes," she murmured as she pushed him back on the bed and began lowering herself along the full length of his body, exploring with her lips as much as with her hands. "It would."

Two, maybe three hours later—Luca didn't know; he'd entirely lost track of time—he slipped out from beneath the covers, trying his best not to disturb Francesca.

All the tiptoeing came to nothing when he picked up his trousers and his belt buckle clattered against the tile flooring. A quick glance toward the bed and he could see one bright blue eye peeking out at him amidst a tangle of blond hair.

"Pia?" she asked.

Luca nodded.

The single word had contained no animosity. Only understanding. His main priority was his niece. Luxurious mornings in bed would never be on his menu, and Fran would have to understand that was his reality.

He swept his fingers through her hair, dropped a kiss on her forehead and left without saying a word.

Outside, he sucked in the night air as if he'd been suffocating.

A night like that...

He wanted more.

Much more.

He tried as best he could to push the thoughts—the desire—away. There was no chance he could make peace with giving in to these precious green shoots, the chance at something new blossoming in a place where he'd thought love would only wither and die.

With his niece to provide for, wanting and having had become two very different things. He could want, but he definitely couldn't have. Fran would just have to understand that.

CHAPTER TEN

A SHOT OF irritation lanced through Luca's already frazzled nerves. Spreadsheets taunted him from his computer screen. Stacks of bills sat alongside ledgers he knew he couldn't reconcile. He barked a hollow laugh into the room.

This must be how his father had felt when his business was failing. Alone. Horrified by the ramifications of what would happen if he admitted his failure to his family. To those he loved the most in the world.

Another peal of hysterics echoed down the corner.

Since when did hydrotherapy sessions contain so much *laughter*?

He pushed back from his desk in frustration. He knew the exact moment. Ever since he'd gone to Francesca. Vulnerable. Heart in hand. Needing help. Needing *her*.

A shot of desire coursed through him and just as quickly he iced it.

Their nights together were…otherworldly. Never before had he met his match as he had with Francesca. The pure alpha male in him loved hearing her call his name as he pleasured her. Loved teasing and taunting just a little longer as she begged him to enter her. Even now, fully clothed, he could conjure up the sensation of Fran's nails scratching along the length of his back as he thrust deeply into her until the pair of them both cried out in a shared ecstasy.

If only he hadn't gone to her to ask for help. Help she'd given willingly. Gladly, even. But it made him feel weak. It ate at his pride and filled him with yet another measure of self-loathing he'd yet to conquer.

He was meant to be shouldering the load. Righting wrongs *he* had set in motion.

Paolo's triumphant cry of "I did it!" pierced through to his consciousness.

Pride was his enemy. The devil on his shoulder drowning out the man he'd buried somewhere deep inside him, who knew having Fran here was exactly what the patients needed. What *he* needed.

The Francesca Effect, the staff were calling it.

Yes, the patients worked hard, but they also laughed and cheered, and a few had even cried in moments of triumph they had never thought they'd achieve.

Like a moth to a flame he found himself drawn to the hydrotherapy room.

He looked through the glass window running the length of the indoor pool and ground his teeth together.

Even in a functional one-piece swimsuit she was beautiful. Her hair was in Heidi plaits, trailing behind her in the water as she faced Paolo in his chair, stretching from side to side of the pool along with him, keeping up a steady flow of encouragement. Silly jokes. Pointing out every time he'd done well. Reached further. Done more. Aimed higher.

Luca pressed his head to the glass and as he did so, Fran turned to him, her blue eyes lighting up and her smile growing even broader.

He wanted to smile, too. His heart pounded in his

chest, demanding some sort of response, yet all he could do was grind his teeth tighter together.

How could he let her know? This beautiful, care-free, intelligent, loving woman to whom he could lay no claim... How could he let her know the simple truth?

He turned away before he could see the questions deepen in her pure blue eyes and strode to his office, slamming the door shut behind him and returning to his desk.

Try as he might, the columns and figures blurred to-gether. He pressed his fingertips to his forehead, trying to massage some sort of meaning into them.

It was pointless, really. No matter which way he rear-ranged them—no matter how many times he added them up—the answer was always the same.

It wouldn't last.

Couldn't last.

And the sooner he came to terms with that, the better.

"How's your grip? Still strong?" Fran wheeled herself around in Pia's wheelchair to the edge of the pool.

Pia looked up at Fran from where she was being towed along the shallow end of the pool's edge and grinned. "I think Freda is doing most of the work here, but I'm still hanging on." She faked letting go of the mop head Fran had rigged up as a steering wheel between her and Freda.

"Ha-ha. Better not let your uncle see that."

"You mean Zio the Thundercloud?"

"Yeah." Fran did her best to stay neutral. "Him."

She and Luca had rigorously stuck to their boundar-ies over the past week.

Lover by night—ridiculously fabulous.

Physio and hydrotherapist by day—so much more re-warding than she'd remembered. Teenagers were a hoot.

And, of course, assistance-dog trainer by afternoon.

Although Pia was doing well, Fran had resorted to in-venting hybrid physio-hydro-canine combo therapies. If the teen kept it up, Fran would be extraneous before long and would be able to go home.

Home.

Three weeks ago it had been all she could dream of. Her dad. Her new business. But now leaving Mont di Mare seemed more punishment than pleasure.

"How are your wheelchair skills coming along?" Pia teased, openly laughing when Fran tried to mimic her teenage charge and pop a wheelie but failed.

"I've still got a way to go to be on par with you."

"You could always get in a car accident that pretty much ruins your life. Then you'd catch up pretty quick," Pia shot back.

From the shocked look on Pia's face Fran knew the teen hadn't meant the words as they'd sounded. Dark. Angry.

"*Scusi*, Francesca. I didn't mean—"

"Hey…" Fran held up her hands. "This is a safe zone." She drew an invisible circle around the pool area, where she knew it would just be the two of them for the next hour or so as Luca and the rest of the staff were still neck-deep in appointments in the main clinic buildings. "You can say whatever you like. Better out than in, right?"

"Anything?" Pia asked incredulously.

"Anything." Fran gave a definitive nod.

What *she* wouldn't have done to have had an older woman in her life when she was growing up. Someone to confide in. To ask those awkward girl questions that adolescence unearthed.

"Do you think I will ever be able to do more in this pool than be dragged back and forth by Freda?" Pia's face shifted from plaintive to apologetic in an instant. "Not that I don't totally love her. Or this. Or being here with you. It's just...sometimes it's really frustrating."

Fran nodded. It was impossible to imagine. She could just step up and out of the wheelchair whenever she chose and dive into the pool. Do a cartwheel. Anything.

She considered Pia for a moment, then focused on the path Freda was taking, back and forth along the length of the pool.

"It's too bad we can't get Edison in there. He would tow you around like a motorboat!"

The second the words were out of her mouth Fran regretted saying them. From the ear-to-ear grin on Pia's face it was more than obvious that to her being pulled around at high speed sounded great.

"That would be amazing! Zio Luca would—"

"Go apoplectic with rage," Francesca finished for her.

"It's not like anyone else is using the pool." Pia splashed a bit of water toward her.

"Yet," Fran intoned meaningfully, lifting her face up to the sun. "But once everyone's properly settled this place will be more popular than the walk-in refrigerator."

"You mean wheel-in, don't you, Fran?" Pia teased.

"Si. Of course. Wheel-in fridge. Either way, I don't think your uncle would be happy to know the pool maintenance guy might be scooping dog hair out of the filters."

"We could do it! *I'd* do it. All I'd have to do is lie on the ground before I get in my chair and just fish it all out. Excellent upper body strengthening opportunity." Pia smiled cheekily. "He would never have to know."

Fran gave her a sidelong glance. "I think you know as well as I do that your uncle is all seeing, all knowing."

She pointed up to the security camera she was praying he wasn't keeping an eye on.

"He's a pussycat, really."

"Mountain lion, more like."

A sexy mountain lion, with far too much weight on his shoulders.

He shouldn't have to do all this alone. If only she could stay. Share the load.

She wheeled the chair around in a few idle circles, unable to stop a sigh heaving out of her chest. Edison appeared with a ball in his mouth, his permanently worried-looking eyebrows jigging up and down above his amber eyes.

"Don't worry, boy," she whispered into the soft fold of his ear. "I'm not sad. I'm...*perplexed*. Wanna play catch?"

Back and forth went the ball and the dog. Back and forth. Just like her thoughts.

It wasn't as if she wanted to win Luca's heart or anything. She just really believed in everything he was doing here at the clinic.

Boundaries.

A sudden frisson swept through her as her thoughts slipped far too easily back to the bedroom. Had she actually bitten into his shoulder last night, when the explosion of their mutual climax had hit the heavens and returned her to earth in thousands of glittery, grinning pieces?

She threw the ball again. Harder this time.

Edison duly loped off. Returned. Totally obedient.

"C'mon, boy. Drop the ball. There's a good boy," she cooed. "You *always* do everything I ask."

Her eyes pinged wide. Was that why she'd switched to dogs? Because they always did what she wanted? That couldn't possibly be what she was hoping for in a man. *Obedience?*

No! Ridiculous. She wanted a man with his own mind, his own interests—but his heart? She wanted that to beat solely for *her*. And no matter how smitten Luca seemed between the hours of 10 p.m. and whenever they'd exhausted each other, she knew his heart was well and truly off-limits.

"Good boy. Drop the ball." This time she threw it extra hard, her eyes widening in horror when she saw where it had landed. At the far end of the very pristine, very new, entirely immaculate swimming pool...now getting dive-bombed by a thrilled Labrador.

Pia was nearly crying with laughter.

"Can he pull me around now, Francesca? *Per favore? Bravo*, Edison! *Vieni qui*."

"No way!" Fran whispered as if it would make the scenario disappear.

She pulled off the sundress she was wearing over her bikini and dove into the pool, as if she would be able to magnetically draw any loose hairs Edison might be leaving in his wake.

"Edison! *Out!*"

"Edison, *vieni qui*!" Pia repeated. More adamantly this time. "You know…" Pia went on slowly, avoiding eye contact with Fran as she spoke, "Zio Luca didn't say *specifically* that I was meant to have just one assistance dog. You said yourself you'd brought two to see which one I hit it off with the best, and, well…it's not like everyone has just *one* best friend, right?"

"It is pretty standard. Having just the one."

"*What* about life up here at Mont di Mare is standard?" Pia appealed.

Fran couldn't help laughing. She knew exactly where Pia was coming from. It *was* otherworldly up here.

She took a few strokes in Pia's direction, to where Edison was merrily paddling around her. She watched as the teen lay back in the water, her slim legs floating up to the surface. Her fingers pitter-patted on the water's surface, and all the while she was humming a pop tune as she worked on her argument. She looked like any normal kid having a float in a pool—if you ignored the harness and pole contraption she was still holding on to, the life vests, and the float around her neck for an extra "just in case."

"Won't Edison miss Freda?" Pia asked eventually. "I mean, they both spend most of their time with me now, so it wouldn't be like keeping both would be that strange."

"What? And leave me all alone?" Fran had meant it as a jest, but the reality of returning to the States alone…

Ugh. Boundaries, Francesca. Boundaries!

She dunked herself under the surface of the water to mask the rush of emotion. She was meant to be Pia's sounding board, not the other way around. She whooshed up and out of the pool, pulled a huge bath towel around her and plonked herself down in Pia's chair, calling Edison out of the pool.

Staying or going, Luca would kill her if he saw a dog in his fancy pool.

"Just remember, Fran, *you* can get up out of that chair anytime you want and just walk away," Pia sternly reminded her. "I'm stuck in it forever."

The words all but ejected Fran straight out of the chair and into the pool.

She looked from Pia to Edison, his furry legs pedaling at the sky as he rolled on the grass, rubbing the pool water off his back. Then to Freda, who always looked as if she was smiling, happy as ever to stand or walk by Pia's side.

The thought of life without Freda and Edison was sobering. But that was how it worked.

You train them, you hand them over, you move on.

Normally she was fine with it. But this time it didn't feel right.

"Don't you think you should try asking?" Pia let go of the mop handle and folded her hands in the prayer position before quickly grabbing it again. "It'd be better coming from you."

"Me?" A cackle of disbelief followed the wide-eyed yeah-right look Fran threw Pia's way. "I think pleading for favors from your uncle is more *your* turf."

Pia made a pouty face, then quickly popped on a smile. "Take me to the edge!"

"What? The far edge?" The one overhanging the sheer drop of the mountain. "Not a chance!"

"I bet Edison would do it if we were here alone," Pia grumped.

"And what makes you think your uncle would be thrilled about you being in the pool on your own."

"That's exactly the point! I wouldn't *be* on my own. Edison could tow me around, and if anything went wrong, Freda could run for help." Pia's features widened, then threatened to crumple. "For once I could feel like a normal kid. Just *once*."

"Pia, I really don't think…"

Once more Pia pressed her hands into the prayer position. "*Per favore*, Francesca. Help the poor little orphan girl on the mountaintop."

"Just the once?" Fran finally conceded.

She knew she was supposed to be the older, wiser person in this scenario. At twenty-nine years old she was hardly old enough to be her mother, but she felt protective of Pia. She could say, hand on her heart, that she loved her. Even if she *was* extra cheeky. Demanding. Unbelievably capable of getting her to take risks she knew Luca would frown upon.

She glanced at the sheer drop at the edge of the infinity pool.

Luca was going to kill her. Well and truly kill her.

"C'mon, you wily minx. I'm going to get you out of here. Let go of the pole and grab hold of my neck."

"I'm not wily!" Pia feigned a hurt look. "I'm...*cunning.*"

"That you are." She reached out to Pia and unclipped the pole from Freda.

"You promised!"

"What exactly did you promise?"

Pia and Fran froze, then slowly shifted their gazes from each other to the pair of leather shoes attached to a familiar pair of long legs, which were, in turn, supporting a terrific torso—lovely clothed or unclothed—topped off by one very unamused face.

"Francesca? What did you promise my niece?"

"I promised to keep her hair dry!" Fran chirped.

"*Si*, Zio. That's exactly what she promised. And to keep me safe and out of harm's way." Pia added, tightening her hold on Fran's neck as she did.

"That's us! Two little safety nuts!" Fran grinned while Pia maintained a frantic nodding, as if it would erase everything else from Luca's mind.

Two inane, grinning bobbleheads, still neck-deep in the pool. Which was another issue. If she stepped out any farther, he would see her breasts had pinged to full Luca-alert position.

She narrowed her gaze and dared a quick scan. Damn, that man was head to toe desirable. Even when he was glowering at her.

"And the dog?" Luca couldn't resist tipping his head toward the Lab merrily paddling around the pool. "Is he part of the safety plan?"

"Absolutely...not..."

Fran slipped Pia's arms more securely around her neck and walked her toward the shallow end of the pool. With each step she took, Luca couldn't help but think he was watching a beach-rescue video. In slow motion.

With that barely there bikini on—

Dio mio.

"What *were* your plans to get Pia out of the pool?" Luca heard the bite in his voice and detested himself for it. But he'd been scared. He'd heard screams and had feared the worst.

Lungs heaving with the effort of reaching the pool to save his niece, he felt the burn as he surveyed the scene now. His niece had been in gales of laughter. All because of Fran. Of course. Francesca wasn't just a ray of sunshine—she was a cascade of light. Wherever she went.

"We actually practiced it a lot at the beginning of the session," Fran said, rattling off a technique she'd seen on the internet.

"Aren't you meant to be studying?" He zeroed in on Pia, feeling less like a loving uncle and more like an officer in the Gulag.

"I finished early. Fran helped me with my trigonometry. And it was such a lovely day..."

"How did you get her in?" Luca asked Fran, not entirely certain he wanted to know.

Pia peeked out from behind Fran's head once again. "I swan-dived."

"You *what*?" His voice dropped in disbelief. "The only way you could have done that is if—"

"I tipped her in," Fran interjected, her expression every bit as stoic as an elite soldier caught going a step too far by the drill sergeant.

"Pia said she knew how to swim—that it was her favorite part of rehab when you were still in Rome—so I tipped her in. And because she's such an amazingly graceful girl she turned it into a swan dive!"

"She could've been—"

"What? Paralyzed?" Pia cut in. "Uncle Luca, it's okay. There is no way Edison, Freda or Fran would've let me drown. Besides, it felt amazing. Like I was whole again."

He looked to Fran, saw her teeth biting down on her lip so hard the flesh paled around it. Then he saw the defiance in her eyes.

C'mon. Do it. I dare you to take away this moment from your niece.

Didn't she realize his niece was the only person he had left in the world, and that to chuck her into a swimming pool without the necessary precautions was sheer madness?

"Don't move. I'll go and get one of the portable hoists. I hope I can trust you to respect my wishes for just a few moments?"

His back stiffened as a peal of nervous giggles followed him when he about-faced and began stomping off. Then it struck him. Fran had done it again. Found exactly the sort of moments he'd been hoping for Pia would have here at Mont di Mare. Happy ones. Discovery. Trying new things. Making the village a home as well as his place of work.

His pace slowed. What sort of life was he giving his niece here? Did he even know what Pia wanted to do when she grew up? When was the last time they'd sat down and eaten a normal dinner together? As a family?

An image of the three of them sitting down—Fran, Pia and Luca—enjoying a meal together put a lift in his step. And then just as quickly weighed it down. They weren't a family. It was just him and Pia, and he was barely succeeding at that. And as for the clinic—the bank was still nipping at his heels, getting ever closer.

When he returned a few minutes later with the hoist he saw Pia on the top step at the side of the pool, tugging herself into her wheelchair with a small grunt and a smiley, "Voilà!" She looked him in the eye as he approached. "See? I didn't need you after all."

He forced a smile, knowing full well it didn't reach his eyes. Not because he wasn't happy for her, but because he was furious with himself for being so blind.

Letting her fend for herself was the only way to build Pia's confidence. It was the entire raison d'être of the clinic. How had he lost sight of the endgame so quickly?

When his eyes met and meshed with Fran's a rush of emotion hit him so hard he could barely breathe. Half of him resented her for being there for his niece. The other half was grateful. If only he'd had a chance to grieve for all that he had lost—not just in the accident, but in the years that followed. His spontaneity. His voracious appetite for experimental treatments. His passion for life. His capacity to love.

Perhaps then he would be whole again.

"Would you like to take Pia back to the house?" Fran finally asked. "I'm happy to bring the hoist back to the clinic."

It was an olive branch. She was trying to bring him

closer to Pia, not divide them. He was grateful for the gesture.

"*Grazie*, Fran. See you tomorrow at the clinic?"

She knew what he was saying. They wouldn't meet tonight. He simply couldn't. Not with the demons he was battling.

"Of course," she replied, her eyes darting away in an attempt to hide the hurt he'd seen in an instant. "Tomorrow at the clinic."

He just caught Pia rolling her eyes at him, then putting her hands out. *Do something! Fix it!* her expression screamed.

But all he was capable of was letting Francesca walk away.

CHAPTER ELEVEN

"Here's the break point."

Luca followed Dr. Murro's finger as he pointed out the T11 vertebra on the X-ray.

"Hard to miss, isn't it?" he replied grimly. "Severed right in two. No chance of recovering function below the waist." Luca shook his head. Off-road vehicles could be dangerous things. "She's lucky the vertebra didn't rupture her aorta."

"Has Francesca done any work with her?"

"I don't think so." Luca shook his head. "She usually submits a report as soon as she's worked with a patient, and I haven't seen one for Maria yet."

"She'll be staying on?"

"Who? Maria? Of course. She's only just arrived."

"Francesca," Dr. Murro corrected.

Ah. That was a more complicated answer.

"The whole staff seem to have really taken to her," Dr. Murro continued.

So have I. Too much.

"She has commitments back in the States, making it impossible."

"Shame. Someone like that—a triple threat—is going to be difficult to replace."

"Triple threat?" He'd not heard that turn of phrase before.

"Physio, hydro and canine therapist in one. She's a league above most. A real asset to Mont di Mare."

"That she is," Luca conceded. "That she is…"

A sharp knock sounded on the exam room door. "Dr. Montovano? It's Cara Bianchi. Francesca has found her out by the meadows, indicating with possible autonomic dysreflexia."

Luca shot from his chair. "Where is she? Have you brought her in?"

"*Si.* One of the doctors is seeing her now, in the Fiore Suite, but it's probably best if *you* take a look."

"On my way." He stopped at the doorway, "Dr. Murro, are you all right to meet with Maria? Talk through her treatment program?"

"Absolutely, Doctor. And if you could send Francesca to meet me when you're done, that'd be great. Well-done for hiring her, by the way. She's a real catch."

Luca nodded, striding out of the office before the scowl hit his lips.

Francesca was more than an asset. She was a woman. One who once you caught hold of, you'd be a fool ever to let go. But he would have to do just that if he was ever going to stand on his own two feet. Provide for his niece. Be the man his family had always believed him to be.

Doctors and nurses were already surrounding Cara on an exam table, where Francesca and a nurse were holding the girl in an upright position.

"She's bradycardic. Blood pressure is one-four-five over ninety-seven," the nurse said as soon as she saw Luca enter.

"Any nasal stuffiness? Nausea?" Luca asked.

"No, but she's complained to Francesca about a head-ache."

He glanced to Fran, who gave a quick affirmative nod.

"When I saw the goose bumps on Cara's knees and felt how clammy her skin was I brought her in here."

"My head is killing me! And my eyes feel all prickly!" Cara wailed from the exam table. "All I wanted to do was lie in the meadow!"

"It's all right… We'll ease the pain. Can we get an ice compress for Cara's face, please?" Luca smiled when he saw that one was being slipped in place before he'd finished speaking. "Autonomic dysreflexia." He gave Fran a grateful nod. "You were right. Can we strap her in and tilt the exam table up?"

"Has anyone checked her urinary bag?"

"Just emptied it. She had a full bladder."

"Bowels need emptying? Any cuts, bruises? Other injuries?"

"Nothing that I could see," said Fran. "But Cara hadn't voided her bladder in a while and was lying down, which I'm guessing exacerbated the symptoms."

She looked to Luca for confirmation. A hit of color pinked up her cheeks when their eyes met.

"Exactly right," Luca confirmed grimly.

It sounded like a simple enough problem, but for a paraplegic it was potentially lethal. Francesca had done well. His eyes met hers and he hoped she could read the gratitude in them.

"That's all it was?" Cara's voice turned plaintive as she scanned the faces in the room. "I just had to pee but it felt like I was going to die?"

"That's the long and short of it, Cara. If you like…" Luca flashed the group a smile, trying to bring some levity to the room, and dropped Cara a quick wink. What he had to say next was a hard bit of information to swallow. Something she'd have to live with for the rest of her life. "Tell the others it was autonomic dysreflexia. Sounds much cooler." The smile dropped from his lips. "But you should also tell them how quickly it can turn critical. All those symptoms are warning signs of a much more serious response."

"Like what?" Her eyebrows shot up.

"Internal bleeding, stroke and even death." He let the words settle before he continued. These kids already had so much to deal with. Worrying about dying simply because their brain couldn't get the message that they needed to pee seemed cruel. Cara had been snowboarding less than a year ago, and now the rest of her life would involve wheelchairs, assistance and terrifying moments like these that, if she were left unattended, might lead to her death.

"You use intermittent catheterization, right?" Luca asked.

Cara nodded, a film of tears fogging her eyes.

Luca turned to the staff. No need for an audience. "I think we're good here. Cara and I might just have a bit of a chat and then…"

He scanned the collected staff including Gianfranco Torino—a GP who had retrained in psychotherapy when he'd suffered his own irrecoverable spinal injury. He, too, would be in a wheelchair for the rest of his life.

"Dr. Torino, would you be able to meet up with Cara later today? Maybe for an afternoon roll around the gardens?"

"Absolutely." Dr. Torino gave Cara a warm smile. "Three o'clock at the pergola? Is that enough time?"

Cara nodded. "*Si*, Dr. Torino. *Grazie*."

"*Prego*, Cara. See you then."

Luca scanned the staff, everyone of them focused on Cara as a unit.

This is the Mont di Mare I imagined.

His eyes lit on Francesca, who lifted her gaze from Cara's hair. She'd been running her fingers through the girl's long dark locks. Soothing. Caressing. When she saw him looking at her and smiled, it felt as if the heat of the sun was exploding in his chest.

Perfection.

And perfectly distracting. Smiles didn't pay bills. Patients did.

He moved his hands in a short, sharp clap. Too loud for the medium-sized exam room. Too late to do anything about it.

"All right, everyone. I think Cara and I need to chat over a couple of things."

Cara reached over her shoulder and grabbed Francesca's hand, shooting Luca an anxious look. "Can Fran stay? She was going to plait my hair—right, Francesca?"

"Ah! You're a hairdresser now?"

He saw the flutter of confusion in Fran's eyes and then the moment she made her decision.

"One of my hidden talents." She gave Cara a complicit wink and gathered her hair together as if it were a beautiful bouquet of wildflowers. "I promise I won't distract you from what you two are talking about."

Her pure blue eyes met his. There were a thousand reasons he should say no, she couldn't stay, and one single reason to say yes. His patient.

The motivation behind everything. Not Fran. Not desire. Not love.

The thought froze him solid for an instant, but quickly he forced himself into motion.

"I may need you to help for a moment before the hair-styling session begins."

"Of course," Fran replied. "Anything you need."

Despite himself, he risked another glance into her eyes and saw she meant it. She wasn't there to take. To demand. To change him. She was simply there to help.

Removing the cold compress from Cara's face, Luca ran a hand across the girl's brow, satisfied the hot flush was now under control. With Fran's help, they triple-checked for bedsores and ensured her clothing was fitting comfortably. A tight drawstring on a pair of trousers could trigger one of these potentially deadly incidents.

Once they were settled, and Fran had magicked a hairbrush from somewhere, he brought over the portable blood-pressure gauge, straddled a stool and wheeled himself over to Cara.

"Arm." He gave her a smile and held out the cuff.

"You already took my blood pressure."

"It's good to do it every five minutes or so when this happens. Here—let's slip your legs over the edge of the table to help your blood pressure. C'mon. Stretch your arm out."

Cara obliged him with a reluctant grin and soon he was pumping up the pressure in the cuff.

"I know you've had a lot to get used to since the accident, and this is another one of those scary learning curves. Basically, your bladder can't tell your brain it's full, so it's best if you have some sort of schedule. Have you ever set up a regular voiding timetable?"

"I did for the couple of months I was back in school, but over the summer I guess I let it lapse a bit." She shot him a guilty look.

"Did your doctors explain what might happen if your bladder was full and you didn't empty it?"

Another guilty look chased up the first. "I forget…"

"They're pretty strong symptoms—as you just found out. I know you've only been here a few days, but if you have a voiding timeline in your schedule it's a good idea to follow it."

"I was just waiting for my parents to go. You know— making the most of the time they were here."

"I thought you were out in the field on your own? That Francesca found you?"

Instinctively, his eyes flicked up to Fran's. The soft smile playing on her lips as she listened to them talk reminded him to do the same. A smiling doctor was much easier to listen to than the furrowed-brow grump he'd been of late.

Cara was remaining stoically tight-lipped.

"Either way, here's what's happening. Autonomic dysreflexia is your body's response to something happening below your injury level. You're a C6, C7 complete, right?"

Cara gave him a wry grin. "Can't get anything past you, can I, Dr. M?"

"Let's hope not, if it means getting you to a place where you're in charge of your own life. So." He gave the reading on the gauge a satisfied nod and took off the cuff. "I'm sure you've heard it before, but this time let it sink in. There are any number of things that can kick off an AD response. Overfull bladder or bowel."

"Ew!"

"I know—it's gross."

"No grosser than picking up dog poop who knows how many times a day!"

Fran's fingers flew to cover her mouth. *Oops!* So much for staying out of the doctor-patient talk!

Cara gave her a toothy grin. One Fran was pretty sure contained a bit of bravura.

"Actually…do you think an assistance dog would be able to remind me?" Cara had switched from doleful teen to bargaining expert.

Ah! *That* was why the teen had asked her to stay. Not for her sure-handed approach to a fishtail braid.

"That's not really my terrain." Luca pressed his lips together. "Francesca?"

Fran shook her head in surprise. Was Luca *including* her in this?

"Sorry, hon. What exactly is it you want to know?"

"If an assistance dog—one like Edison, maybe—were to help me, couldn't he remind me of things?"

Fran's instinct was to look to Luca, seek guidance. But to her surprise he just smiled, then widened and raised his hands, as if opening the forum to include her.

She gulped. This was… This was getting *involved*. Becoming interwoven in the fabric of things here on a level she'd told herself was a danger zone. A little dog training here. A bit of physio there. But advising a patient…?

"Francesca?" Luca prompted. "This is your area of expertise."

Dropping her gaze from his, she stared at the plait her fingers was weaving by rote and started speaking.

"Of course assistance dogs can certainly respond to alarms, and help you to remain upright in your wheelchair if you were ever to slump down. They can do a lot. But this sounds to me like something you and Dr. Montovano had better work out."

"But couldn't a dog have told you if I was dead or dying?"

"You mean when I found you out in the field? Absolutely. It would've barked. Tried to get someone to come and see you straightaway."

"Like Lassie?" Cara's voice squeaked with excitement. "If you hadn't found me then a dog could have saved my life!"

"Well…" Fran's fingers finished off the plait and she swirled a tiny elastic band she'd dug out of her pocket onto the end.

She'd overstepped the boundaries before. She really didn't want to do it again.

"Cara, you're with us for the rest of the summer, right?" Luca interjected. *Mercifully.*

Cara nodded.

"How about you and Fran spend a bit of time with Pia's dogs—if it's all right with Pia, of course. See how you go. I'm sure assistance dogs suit some people and aren't quite right for others. Am I right, Francesca?"

She'd expected to see some sort of triumph in his eyes. A way to catch her out. But there was nothing there but kindness. Possibility. Respect.

And for one perfect moment she was lost in the dark chocolate twinkle holding her rapt like a… Ha! The irony. Like a giddy teen.

Her phone buzzed. She glanced at the screen and frowned. Her father didn't normally ring this early.

"Sorry, I've just—"

Luca waved her apologies away. "I think Cara and I have plenty to talk about."

She gave Cara a quick wave, then accepted the call, closing the door softly behind her as she went.

"Si, Papa? Va tutto bene?"

CHAPTER TWELVE

"GOT A MINUTE?"

Fran looked up to find Luca at her doorway, striking the pose that had reduced her to a pool of melted butter a handful of weeks ago—arm resting on the low sling of the beam above her door frame, body outlined by the setting sun.

If she knew how, she'd let out a low whistle of appreciation and give him a one-liner an old-time Hollywood starlet would envy.

Somehow she found her voice. "I was just opening a bottle of wine. Fancy a glass?"

Luca didn't answer straight away, his eyes narrowing slightly as if inspecting her for ulterior motives. Which only succeeded in making her think of all the illicit things she could do with him right here and now, if only he'd duck his head, step inside her cottage and kick the door shut behind him.

Desire flared up hot and intense within her.

Bad brain. Naughty thoughts. Quit staring at the sexy doctor.

"*Grazie*. I'd love a glass of wine."

Good, brain. Excellent thoughts. Run to the bedroom to check it doesn't look like a hurricane has hit it.

"Mind if we sit out here? On the bench?"

What? Does not compute.

Then again, not a lot of what passed between them computed. Their tempestuous nights of lovemaking chased up by…absolutely nothing. No talks. No explanations. Just complicated silences.

Perhaps a talk was exactly what they needed.

"Here." Fran threw him a couple of pillows from the sofa. "Makes it comfier."

She pulled on a light sweater, grabbed another glass and cascaded an arc of gorgeous red wine into the goblet, all the while rearranging her features into something she hoped looked like casual delight that Luca had chosen sitting outside on a bench over ripping off his clothes.

"Everything all right with your phone call?" he asked.

"Mmm, yes." She quickly swallowed down a spicy gulp of Dutch courage, then topped up her glass. "It was my father."

"All's going well on the home front?"

"Very. So good, in fact, he'd like to come over."

She stepped outside the cottage in time to see Luca's eyes widen in surprise.

"I know. It freaked me out, too. My dad's never visited me before. Must be all these video calls we've had. I've been showing him Mont di Mare."

"Oh?" Luca's tone was unreadable. "Did he like what he saw?"

"Very much."

She looked up into Luca's eyes as she handed him his glass. His hand brushed hers, lingering just a fraction of a second longer than necessary, and with the connection a rush of heated sparks raced up her arm and circled around her heart.

"How did your day go with Pia?"

Luca stared deep into his wineglass before taking a

thoughtful draught, tasting it fully before swallowing it down.

Had he felt it, too?

"Really well," Fran managed as nonchalantly as she could, tucking her feet up under her on the broad wooden bench. "She and the dogs have a whale of a time together."

"I meant as regards the training."

Killjoy! It wasn't her fault that their being together made them all fizzy and full of lust and desire and... and other things.

"Getting along with the dogs is part of the training," Fran began carefully. "If they don't sync—you know, make a love match as it were—the relationship isn't going to work out."

"A love match?"

"For lack of a better turn of phrase," Fran mumbled. Could she be digging herself into a bigger hole? It wasn't as if she—*oh, no.*

She looked at him, then away and back again, before realizing what had been happening to her for these past few weeks.

She had fallen in love with Luca. It was mad. And foolish. And totally never going to happen. But—

Did he feel the same way?

She turned to him, seeking answers, only to catch Luca's gaze dropping to her mouth as her lips grazed the edge of her wineglass. An urge to throw caution to the wind took hold of her. Why shouldn't she just go for it? Fling her glass away and climb onto his lap so he could claim what was already his?

His lips parted.

For an instant she was certain she could see it in Luca's eyes, too. The exact same exhilarating rush of realization that he'd found love in the least likely of places. With the least likely of people.

He hesitated.

Was he...? Was he about to tell her he loved her, too?

"What are the actual *practical* things Pia is taking away from this? What, *precisely*, are you enabling her to do by having a dog?"

Fran's heart plummeted, finding itself on all too familiar terrain. She was a solitary girl, seeking her place in the world, only to realize she'd read the wrong page. *Again.*

She scrunched her eyes tight, conjuring up an image of Freda and Edison. She could do with a dose of canine cuddles right now.

"If you'd been spending any time with Pia, you probably would've noticed for yourself," she snapped.

Luca's eyes widened at the level of heat in her voice.

Tough. You just broke my heart.

She looked away, drew in a deep lungful of mountain air and forced it out slowly before continuing.

"Pia and Freda have already mastered a lot of the drop-and-retrieve tasks that will help in her day-to-day life. Right now we're working on Freda responding to very specific verbal commands."

"Like what?" Luca asked—with genuine interest rather than the disdain she'd been expecting. *Good.* At least she'd made some sort of a mark.

Ha! Take that, you doubting...sexy Italian, you.

"Freda can go and get other patients, for example. By name. Scent, really. It's amazing how quickly they learn who is who."

"Why would Pia want her to fetch other patients?"

"Oh...I don't know." Fran took a big gulp of wine before answering that one. "Maybe she's enjoying having some people to spend time with. Friends."

"What would she—" Luca began, then stopped himself, his jaw tensing as his lips pressed together and thinned.

Fran gulped down the rest of her wine, then stood up, hands on hips, to face Luca.

"It may not be my place to say this, but you're letting your niece grow up without you. Take it from me. Once that opportunity is gone, it's hard to claw it back."

A complication of emotions crossed Luca's face as he looked up at her. As if he was having a fight with himself.

"You're right. It's not your place."

Something deep within her flared, hot and fierce.

"That may be so, but let me tell you this. Crush the hearts of all the women you want, Luca Montovano. I'll be fine. *We'll* be fine. But Pia…? You're all she has. You lose this chance to show her you love her and you might lose her for good."

Luca looked away, a searing blast of emotion pounding the breath out of his chest in one sharp, unforgiving blow.

Lose Pia?

Unthinkable.

And what had Fran meant about crushing hearts? Marina wasn't crushed—

"I'll be fine," she'd said.

Did Fran *love* him? Had she invested her heart in those nights they had spent together? Nights he hadn't acknowledged since…since she had become a vital part of his work team. One of the people he kept at arm's length in preparation for the bank's inevitable foreclosure.

He knew she enjoyed sparring with him, working with

him—but love? It wasn't something he had ever allowed himself to consider. Not with so much at stake.

He looked back at her, saw her eyes blazing with indignation. The fury of a child who had been where Pia was now. The rage of a woman who loved a man who could never love her in return.

He pushed himself up to standing after placing his drained glass on the floor and faced her. "You're a very brave woman, Francesca Martinelli."

She shifted her feet, eyes held wide-open as they had been on the very first day they'd met. When she'd been the only one courageous enough to stop her friend from doing something she'd regret forever.

"You never shy away from hard truths, do you, Francesca?"

She gave her head a little shake in agreement.

Luca couldn't help but give a self-effacing laugh. "I suspect moments like these are why Beatrice always speaks so highly of you. Why she insisted you come up here. She said you'd be good for me."

"She did?" Fran's eyes brightened, endearing her to him more than he should allow.

"Often," he said. "And with great affection."

He fought the urge to reach out and touch Fran. Stroke a finger along the length of her jawline. Smooth the back of his hand along the downy softness of her cheek.

"That's good," Fran whispered.

Whether she was referring to Beatrice or to the frisson fizzing between them, Luca couldn't tell. How it had shifted from rage to zingy chemistry, he didn't know, but it had.

Luca took a step back, intentionally breaking the moment in two, and gave his thoughts over to Beatrice—his dear friend who'd all but had the world ripped out from under her feet and yet had remained true, kind. A loving friend who had never, even in her darkest hour, withdrawn her emotions as he so often did. Barring his heart from the aches and pains that loving someone entailed.

"If you don't mind me saying something…" Fran began tentatively.

"Why stop now?" He opened his palms. An invitation for her to continue.

Fran blushed, but continued, "Marina didn't really seem your type. Or deserve you, for that matter."

Before he thought better of it, he asked, "And what exactly is it that *I* deserve?"

They both stopped and stared at each other in a moment of mutual recognition. Of course Francesca was a better choice. The natural choice.

A choice he didn't have the freedom to make.

"Marina just seemed… She seemed to be after something more…*fantasy*. Like in a fairy tale. With cocktails and fast cars."

"That sounds about right," Luca conceded. "You're not like that, though, are you?"

Fran squirmed under his gaze and he didn't blame her. He didn't have the ability to disguise the desire he knew was burning in his eyes. But he couldn't offer her what she deserved. His heart.

He turned to face the view, breaking a moment that would only have led to more heartache. "It's probably just as well we're talking about my relationship failures."

"Why's that?" Fran looked away, then dropped down onto the bench, carefully rearranging the pebbles at her feet with her toe.

"I know my behavior over the past few weeks or so has been…confusing, to say the least."

"Are you saying our being together was a mistake?"

Defensiveness laced her words and tightened the folding
of her arms across her chest.

"No. No, *chiara*." He joined her on the bench and
reached out a hand to cup her chin, so that she could see
straight into his heart when he spoke. "Being with you
was...bittersweet."

She swallowed. He forced himself to hold his ground,
letting his hand shift from her chin to her arms, which he
gently unlaced, taking both of her hands in his.

"I liked the idea of having a summer romance with
you."

"Past tense?" she asked, with her usual unflinching
desire to hear the truth.

"Yes." He owed it to her.

"I thought...I thought you enjoyed being with me."

Little crinkles appeared at the top of her nose as the
sparks in her eyes flared in protest. A swell of emotion
tightened in his throat. "I did. More than I should have,
given the circumstances."

"Which are...?" Francesca barely got the words out
before choking back a small cry of protest.

His fingers twitched and his hands balled into fists.
He didn't want to cause her pain. Far from it.

"You said yourself you have to go home."

"Not for another few weeks!"

"Francesca, Mont di Mare may not *be* here in a few
weeks."

A silence rang between them so powerfully Francesca
felt her skin practically reverberate with the impact of
his words.

"What do you mean?"

"The bank." He spat the word out as if it were poison,
then swept an arm along the length of the village. "The

bank will own all of this in a few weeks if I don't turn things around."

She shook her head as if he'd just spoken in a foreign tongue. "I don't understand…"

"You don't need to." He bit the words out one by one, as if he were actually shouldering the weight of the mountain as he did so. "My focus needs to be entirely on the clinic, and what little time I have left in my day—as you so rightly pointed out—I need to give to Pia. She's all I have."

"You know you could have more," Fran asserted.

"Only to have you disappear at the end of the summer, along with Mont di Mare?" He didn't pause to let Fran answer, and his voice softened as he offered her what little consolation he could. "I've experienced enough loss to last a lifetime, *amore*. I don't think I could bear any more."

A dog's bark filtered into the fabric of the night sounds. It reminded him that he'd delivered the death knell to any future between them. The least he could do was soften the blow.

"I meant to say the reason I was asking so much about the dogs is that after our session with Cara a couple of other patients were asking whether or not they might have one, too. If it suits you, you could look into supplying them with assistance canines before the summer is out."

Fran didn't know whether to be elated or furious, given the circumstances. Shell-shocked was about as close as she could come.

Luca was about to lose the entire village and still his thoughts were on his patients?

Her heart bled for him, and then just as quickly tightened in a sharp twist of anguish.

Why couldn't he afford *her* the same courtesy?

Take a risk.

Chance his heart on love.

She stared at him, searching his dark eyes for answers.

How could he just stand there like that? All business and attention to detail when everything he'd worked so hard for was slipping away.

Wasn't he full of rage? Of fight? *Why* wouldn't he let her love him? Take the blows of an unfair world alongside him?

She stared at Luca, amazed to see the light burning in his eyes turn icy cold.

Perhaps he was right. He was giving her a chance to cut her losses. Preserve what was left of her heart. Do her job, then get on with her life—just as she'd planned.

She forced on her most businesslike tone. He wanted facts? He could *have* facts.

"You know it takes more than a couple of weeks to find the right dogs, let alone train them up, right? It requires skill. Precision. Plus, I adopt dogs from local shelters, so sometimes there are additional factors to consider. What if the patient doesn't take to the dog and I can't bring it back to the States? I could hardly return it to the shelter afterward, could I? Having given it a glimpse of another life?"

Luca stared at her. Completely unmoved.

Fran continued. "Dogs are loyal, even if people aren't, and I don't play emotional bingo. With anyone."

It was vaguely satisfying to finally see a glint of discord in Luca's eyes.

Vaguely.

There was no glory in one-upping a man whose world was about to collapse in on him.

She bent and picked up his wineglass from the ground,

then took a definitive step toward her doorway before turning to address him again.

"I *will* speak with your administrator about patients looking to work with an assistance dog and see if there's someone local who can be brought in. It would be foolish to invest in something I won't be able to see through to the bitter end. If you'll excuse me?"

She scooted around Luca and into her cottage before she could catch another glimpse of those beautiful dark eyes of his, silently cursing herself, her life—anything she could think of—as she shut the door behind her.

Leaning against the thick, time-worn oak, she let a deep sigh heave out of her chest.

As painful as it was for her to admit, Luca was right. There was too much at stake for him to worry about foolish things like a summer romance. She was going home. She'd promised her father—just as he had promised her.

The only thing she could do now was follow the advice she'd given to Luca. Spend her time building a life she wouldn't regret.

A flicker of an idea came to her, but just as quickly as it caught and flared brightly, she blew it out.

She wasn't ready to ask her father for help. Not yet.

But a talk…

She could do with a talk right now.

She swiped at the number and smiled as the phone began to ring.

Before, she had always turned to Bea, but now, hearing her father's voice brighten when he picked up the phone, she let gratitude flood into her heart that, step by step, they were forging a real relationship.

CHAPTER THIRTEEN

LUCA FROWNED. HE'D caught a glimpse of her. As per usual, no matter how stealthily Fran passed, he always knew when she was near. It was a sixth sense he'd grown all too aware of.

He glanced up at the clock. It was past seven. A lovely evening. Well after rehab hours. The residents were all back in their villas, Pia was tucked up with the dogs, watching a film, and here he was hunkered over a pile of papers, brow furrowed, one hand ramming his hair away from his forehead, the other spread wide against the mahogany sheen of the large desk he commanded. Taut. Ready for action. Poised like a reluctant but honorable admiral, helming a ship when duty called.

"Fran!"

He called out her name before he thought better of it. Unlike Francesca, who, true to her word, had maintained an entirely professional demeanor in the weeks following their talk, Luca had behaved like a bear with a sore head.

A golden halo of hair appeared, then her bright eyes peeped around the edge of his door frame like a curious kitten—tempted, but not quite brave enough to enter the lion's lair.

Luca gazed at her for a moment, just enjoying the chance to drink her in. Those blue eyes of hers were skidding around his office as if trying to memorize it. Or maybe that was just him hoping. It wouldn't be long now before she left.

Her loose blond curls rested atop the soft slope of her bare shoulders. The tiny string straps of her sundress reminded him of…too much.

He pushed the pile of papers away, against his better judgment, and rose. "Fancy a walk? I could do with some fresh air."

She shot him a wary look, then nodded. Reluctantly.

They strolled for a few minutes in a surprisingly comfortable silence. Strands of music, television and laughter ribboned out from the villas along with wafts of home-cooked food.

Fran broke the silence. "That smells good."

"My mother used to call the scents up here 'the real Italy,'" Luca laughed softly at the memory.

"In my house that was store-bought macaroni and cheese!" Fran huffed out a laugh that was utterly bereft of joy.

Her response to his throwaway comment was a stark reminder to Luca that he did have blessings to count. Proper childhood memories. Family, laughter, love and joy.

"So what were they? Those scents of the real Italy?" Fran asked.

"Oh, let's see…" He stopped and closed his eyes for a moment, letting the memories comes to him. "Torn basil leaves. The ripest of tomatoes. Freshly baked focaccia. *Dio*, the bread alone was enough to bring you to your knees. Signora Levazzo!" The memory came to him vividly. "Signora Levazzo's focaccia was the envy of all the villagers. She had a secret weapon."

"Which was…?" Fran asked.

"Her son's olive oil. He had a set of olive trees he always used. Slightly more peppery than anyone else's. No one knows how he did it, but—oh!" He pressed his fingers to his lips and kissed them. *"Delicioso!"*

"Sounds lovely."

He didn't miss the hint of wistfulness in her voice. Or the pang in his heart that she hadn't enjoyed those simple but so-perfect pleasures in her own childhood. From the smattering of comments he'd pieced together, she hadn't had much of a childhood at all.

"They were unforgettable summers." Luca looked up to the sky, unsuccessfully fighting the rush of bitterness sweeping in to darken the fond memories. "And to think I told them to sell it all."

"Who? Your family?" Fran's brow crinkled.

He nodded. "We spent all our summers here. Well…" He held up his index finger. "Everyone but me once I'd turned eighteen."

"What happened then?" Fran asked, her eyes following the line of his hand as he indicated that they should follow a path leading to the outer wall of the village.

"The usual things that happen to an eighteen-year-old male. Girls. Motorcycles. University. Medicine."

Fran laughed, taking a quick, shy glimpse up toward him. "I don't think most eighteen-year-old males are drawn to medicine."

"Well…I always like to be different."

"You definitely are that," Fran said, almost swallowing the words even as she did. "And it was plastics you went into?"

"Reconstructive surgery," he corrected, then amended

his brusque answer. "I did plastics to feed my taste for the high life. Reconstructive surgery to feed my soul."

Fran shot him a questioning glance.

"I did a lot of pro bono cases back then. Cleft palates. Children who'd been disfigured in accidents. That sort of thing."

He felt Fran's eyes travel to his scar and turned away. He'd never remove his scar. Not after what he'd done.

Abruptly Fran stopped and knelt, plucking at a few tiny flowers. She held them up when he asked if she was making a posy.

"Daisy chain," she explained, turning her focus to joining the flowers together. "It's fun. You should try it."

"I don't do *fun*," Luca shot back.

"I know." Fran pressed her heels into the ground and rose to her full height. "That's why I said it."

Luca turned away to face the setting sun.

He shouldn't have to live like this, she thought. All stoic, full of to-do lists and health-and-safety warnings. He was a kind, generous man who—when he dared to let the mask drop—was doing his best to stay afloat and do well by his niece. And failing at both because he insisted upon doing it alone.

She placed the finished daisy chain atop her head, then reached out to grab his hand before he strode off beyond her reach. His heart might not be free to love her, but he didn't have to do this alone.

"Talk to me."

A groan of frustration tightened Luca's throat around his Adam's apple. If he hadn't squeezed her fingers as he made the animalistic cry, she would have left immediately. But when his fingers curled around hers and pressed into the back of her palm, she knew it was his way of doing the best he could—the only way he knew how.

"C'mon…" She tried again. "Fair is fair. You got *my* life story on my first day here."

When she sent him a playful wink she received a taut grimace in place of the smile she'd hoped to see.

"I was looking after my niece. Ensuring you weren't some lunatic Bea had sent my way."

Fran clucked her tongue. "First of all, Bea would never do that. And, second of all, I think you know I've encountered enough crazy in my life for you to feel safe in the knowledge I will pass no judgment when I hear your story."

Was that…? Had he just…? Was that the hint of a smile? No. He gave a shake of his head.

Frustration tightened in her chest. What would it take to get this man to trust her?

"Listen. Of all the people up here in this incredible, wonderful center of healing you've created, you seem to be the only one not getting any better."

She ignored his sharp look and continued.

"I'm probably the only one here who knows exactly what it's like to butt heads with their own destiny. My dad's due any day now and I'm already quaking in my boots. Please…" She gave his hand a tight squeeze. "Just lay your cards on the table and see what happens."

A rancorous laugh unfurled from deep within him. "Oh, *chiara*. If only you knew how apt your choice of words was…"

"Well, I *would* know if you told me." Despite all her efforts to rein in her emotions, she couldn't help giving the ground a good stamp with her foot.

Luca arced an eyebrow at her. "It's not a very nice story."

"Nor is mine. It's not like I'm made of glass, Luca. I'm flesh and blood. Just like you."

Luca's lips remained firmly clamped shut.

"You've already had my body!" she finally cried out in sheer frustration. "What do you *want*? Blood?"

CHAPTER FOURTEEN

LUCA WHEELED ON FRAN, his features turning dark, almost savage in their intensity. "I didn't ask for anything from you, *chiara*. Not one kiss. Not one cent. Remember that when you're gone."

Shock whipped anything Fran might have said in response straight out of her throat. She felt her mouth go dry and, despite the warmth of the summer's evening, she shivered as the blood drained from her face when he continued.

"Don't think I haven't seen it."

"Seen what?" Fran looked around her, as if the answer might pop out from behind a bush. She was absolutely bewildered.

"I *know* how you speak of Mont di Mare. How you've made this place into some sort of Shangri-la. A place where nothing can go wrong. Where everything is perfect and rose-colored. You don't get to do that. Not without knowing the facts."

Luca drew in a sharp breath, the air near enough slicing his throat as it filled his lungs.

What the hell?

After a summer of holding it all in, he couldn't contain his rage any longer.

Losing Fran, the clinic—perhaps even Pia if she saw the shell of a man he'd turned into—was more than he could take.

He began pacing on the outcrop where they'd stopped. And talking. Talking as if his life depended upon it.

"Thanks to my father's time at the poker tables, I am in debt up to my eyeballs. Worse. Drowning."

It was an admission he'd never made aloud.

He was shocked to see compassion in Fran's eyes when he'd been so brutal. Even more, they bore no pity.

It was what he had feared most. The pitying looks. He'd had enough of those at the funeral. The funeral in which he had buried his mother, his father, his sister and brother-in-law all in one awful, heart-wrenching day. A day he never wanted to remember, though he knew slamming the door shut on those memories only left them to fester. To rear their ugly heads as they were doing now.

He glanced across at Fran again. Surely she would shrink away from him at some point. As the facts of the story began to sink in. As the knowledge that *he* was to blame for everything that had come his way became clear.

Astonishingly, she seemed more clear-eyed and steady than he had ever seen her. As if his lashing out at her had been an unwelcome shock, but not unexpected.

"How did you open the clinic without assets?"

Fran's question pulled him back to the facts—however unsavory they were to confront.

"I had saved a fair amount when I working in Rome."

Her eyebrows lifted in surprise.

"Plastic surgery brings in a lot of money when you're willing to put in the hours. That, and some of the doctors here are actually operating as private practices, so they came with their own equipment. Thanks to Bea,

I learned about and applied for a few grants. Historic building restoration and the like. The rest…" He swallowed down the sour memories of learning just how far into penury his father had sunk. "Let's just say what's left of my soul belongs to the devil."

"I doubt that's true, Luca. You're too good a man to compromise your principles."

Surprisingly, Fran's face was a picture of earnestness rather than horror. As if she held out hope that the clinic could still be saved.

"Not me—my father. But I'm sure I can shoulder a large portion of the blame for that, as well. To cut a long story short—if I don't make a profit from the clinic very, very soon it will go to Nartoli Banking. My father leveraged the place."

"What will happen?"

"They'll repossess it." The emotion had drained from his voice now. "In a few weeks, most likely. Sell it to an investor, who will most likely raze the village, turn the site into a modern hotel. *Exclusive*, of course," he added with an embittered laugh.

He thought of Mont di Mare—the historic cottages and stone buildings, the gardens and archways—all of it being obliterated to make way for a glitzy glass-and-steel hotel aimed at the world's rich and careless…

"Is it essential to have the clinic here?" she asked. "I mean, it's obviously beautiful, and just the view alone is healing, but…could you not have set up the clinic in Rome?"

Fran's voice was soft. Nonjudgmental. She wasn't accusing him of making the wrong decision, just trying to paint a picture. She wanted to understand.

"Revitalizing the village had always been my sister and mother's dream," he finally admitted.

"As a clinic?"

He shook his head. "A holiday destination, summer homes—that sort of thing. They even toyed with the idea of trying to revamp it into a living, working village. One with specialized craftsmen—and women," he added quickly, when he saw Fran's lips purse and then spread into a gentle smile at his correction. "Similar ideas to what you had, minus the patients. A place where crafts-people could live and create traditional works of art and wares. Do you know how hard it is to find a genuine blacksmith these days?"

Fran shook her head, then quirked an eyebrow. "About as hard as finding world peace?"

He laughed. Couldn't help it. And was grateful for the release.

Fran lowered herself onto a broad boulder, her legs swinging over the edge as she looked out into the valley below.

Hands on his hips, he scanned the outlook, fully aware that this was most likely one of the last days he could call the view his own.

"This is the first time I've heard you speak about your family," Fran said when he eventually sat down alongside her.

"Pia is my family. I don't even deserve *her*."

He looked across in time to see Fran shake off his words, the hurt he'd caused because he wouldn't—*couldn't*—love her, too.

"I just meant—"

"I know what you meant," he cut in harshly. "I'm sorry, Fran. I know you're all about healing old wounds, making amends with your father and all that, but it's too late for me."

"How do you know that?"

He saw something in her then. A steely determination to see this through with him, no matter how ugly.

"You want the whole story?"

She nodded.

"All right—well, the beginning's pretty easy. Happy childhood. Wonderful mother. Doting father. They would've loved me to take up a bit more of the whole Baron Montovano thing, but they never pressed when they saw medicine was my passion. My sister and mother looked after things here. Had the vision. My father was a proud man. Passionate and very much in love with my mother. A few years ago, when his business ventures started going south along with the rest of the world's, he went into a panic."

"About what?"

"He became convinced he was going to die before my mother."

"Was he sick?" Fran asked.

"No." He corrected himself. "Or not that I was aware of. He and I weren't exactly close by then, and even if I'd asked him, he wouldn't have come to me for a medical exam."

"How do you know that?"

"Because he told me." Luca scraped his hand against the sharp edge of the stone he sat upon, not caring if it lacerated his skin. The cut would hurt less than the words his father had shouted in rage that night at the casino.

"You are the last person I would come to for help. The last person in the world."

"My mother and my sister were his world. He would've done anything for them."

"I bet the same was true for you."

"Don't speak of what you don't know, *chiara*. Do you know how he showed his love? His loyalty to his family?

By taking to the craps table. The poker table. Baccarat. Anything to try to scrape back the money he had lost in business. But instead of securing a healthy nest egg, he lost. Lost it all."

Fran's fingers flew to cover her mouth, but to her credit she didn't say a word.

"Just over two years ago I received a call from a casino in Monaco, asking if I could come and collect him. His pockets were empty and it was either me bailing him out or they'd put him in prison for the night."

He looked up to the sky, completely unadulterated by city lights, and soaked it in.

"I drove from Roma straight to Florence, where my mother and sister were. We decided to all go together. Show our support."

He kept his gaze on the sky. There was no chance he could look into Fran's eyes and get through this part of the story without completely breaking down.

"So we all climbed into the car and drove through the night to go and pick up my wayward father in Monte Carlo."

"You *drove*?" Fran asked incredulously.

"The things you do for love," Luca answered softly. He would have done anything for his father. Walked there if he'd needed to. Oh! How he wished he'd walked.

"What happened when you reached him?"

"He was furious at first. Blaming everything on me. For abandoning the family."

"By working in medicine?" Fran shook her head, as if trying to make sense of it all. "Didn't he know about the charity work you did?"

"No." Luca scraped his other hand along the rough surface of the granite. "It didn't suit my image for people to know, so I never really talked about it."

He tugged a hand through his hair, grateful for the deepening darkness. With any luck, it was hiding the waves of emotion crossing his face at the memory of his father eventually breaking down. Sobbing with relief and sorrow at the pain he had brought to his own family.

"Then we all piled back into my car." He laughed at the memory. They'd been jam-packed in that thing. Like sardines, his mother had kept saying. A motley crew, they'd been. Tearful. Laughing. Up and down the emotional roller coaster until they had all sagged with fatigue.

"Pia, you will be unsurprised to hear, was ever the diplomat. She kept everyone talking about what we were going to make for dinner when we got back to Italy. And it was somewhere around a very vibrant discussion about eggplant parmigiana—"

Luca stopped. This was the hardest part. Pieces of information still only came to him in fragments. His hands on the steering wheel. Entering the tunnel. The articulated truck crossing the median strip—

Mercifully, Pia's memory of the accident had never returned. He prayed, for her sake, that it never would.

"The truck driver must've fallen asleep. That route is renowned for it. Up and over the mountains. Lots of tunnels. We were all tired, too. I'd been driving all day. All night. It was why we'd forced ourselves to keep talking, inventing ridiculous recipes to try when we got home."

Luca felt his voice grow jagged with emotion. Each word became weighted in his chest, as if the words themselves were physical burdens he'd been carrying all these years.

"He just careened straight into us. There was nothing I could do!" The words scraped against his throat as though they were being torn from his chest.

Without even noticing her moving, he suddenly felt

Francesca's arms around him, and after years of holding back the bone-shaking grief of loss—nearly his entire family gone in one sickeningly powerful blow—he wept.

Luca hardly knew how much time had passed when at long last his breath steadied and the reddened edges of his eyes dried.

Fran had not said a single word through his outpouring. No trite placations. No overused sayings to try to soothe away a pain that could never be fully healed. Although now his silent grief had become a sorrow shared. It was Fran's gift to him. He could see it in her eyes, glistening with the tears she had not let herself shed, as he wept in the silvery, ethereal light of the moon.

"So that's where this came from?" Fran reached out and gently ran her finger along his scar.

He nodded, catching her hand beneath his own. He'd never thought of it as disfiguring. More as one of life's cruel reminders that he had debts to pay—both literal and figurative.

"If there's anything I can do—" Fran began, stopping abruptly when he dropped her hand as if it had scalded him.

Her touch hadn't. But her words had.

After all that didn't she see this was *his* burden to bear? His cross to carry alone?

"You've done more than enough, Francesca."

She blinked, and something he couldn't quite read had changed in her eyes when she opened them again. "I hope you're saying that in a good way."

"As best I know how. Now..." He pushed himself up, offering her a hand so that she could rise more easily from their mountainside perch. "I'd best be off. See my niece. *Buonasera.*"

He left a bemused Francesca at her doorway, not daring to let himself dip down and give her cheek a kiss. He'd said too much. Bared too much of his heart.

He had three minutes—the length of the walk between her cottage and his own—to pull himself back together. Make a man out of himself again before he saw Pia.

How would he tell her he was going to lose this place to the bank?

Again, his eyes returned to the stars, searching for answers.

God willing, he would never have to say a word.

Fran pulled a blanket over her shoulders and curled up in the window seat. The way her mind was buzzing, sleep was going to be a hard-won commodity. Nearly as impossible as it had been to say good-night to Luca.

Never before had she been so moved as when she and Luca had held each other and he'd finally given in to the years of grief he'd held pent up inside him.

If only—

No.

She gave herself a sharp shake, willing the tears forming in her eyes to disappear. If Luca could be so strong under such heartrending circumstances, she would strive to be the same. Never before had she held someone in such high regard. Never before had she felt such compassion, such love, for one man.

Even if he couldn't return her love he'd shown her the power of sacrifice. Sacrifices she was willing to make even if it cost her her heart.

Shivering a bit, she pulled the blanket closer around her shoulders, willing her body to recapture the sense of warmth she'd felt when she had held Luca.

She had half a mind to call Bea, desperate to brainstorm with someone. Come up with something, *anything* that would help save Mont di Mare from the bank. But Bea had enough on her plate without this to worry about.

Then the lightning-bolt moment came.

She *did* know one person whose entire life had been fueled by the betrayal of another. Who had poured his every energy into exacting revenge by succeeding in his own right.

Her tummy lurched, then tightened as her nerves collected into one jangling ball in her chest, but she picked up her phone anyway.

Courage.

That was what Luca had. In spades.

Strength.

She dialed the number. Took a deep breath…

Forgiveness.

Luca had so many reasons to let his heart turn black, and through everything all she had seen was compassion and—

"*Si, pronto?*"

Love.

"*Papa, è Francesca. Va bene?*"

CHAPTER FIFTEEN

"THAT WAS AN excellent session, Giuliana. Are you pleased with your progress?"

Luca took a seat beside the girl as she wheeled her chair into the shade of the pergola after Dr. Torino had headed back to the gym.

"Si." Her eyes glistened with pride. "All the therapists and doctors here have been amazing. I can't believe how quickly I've gained in strength. Don't let Fran go back to America."

The smile dropped from his eyes. "I'm afraid I don't have much control over that."

"I'm sure if you asked her…"

Luca tsk-tsked and shook his head. "We're not talking about Fran right now—we're talking about you and your progress."

He didn't want Fran to go. But he was hardly going to beg her to stay on a sinking ship.

"Dai. Facci vedere i muscoli."

Despite his grim mood, Luca smiled as Giuliana pushed back her T-shirt and flexed her slender bicep.

He gave it an appreciative squeeze. *"Va bene*, Giuliana. You'll be winning arm wrestling matches soon."

This was the fun part. The satisfying part of being a doctor. Happy patients. Positive results.

"You're not finding the full days of rehab too tiring?"

Giuliana gave the exasperated sigh of a teenager. "No more than I'm supposed to!"

"Excellent. You're a star patient."

Giuliana giggled, waving away his praise. "That's not hard when there's only five of us. Besides—" she fixed Luca with a narrow-eyed gaze "—I have it on good authority you say that to everyone."

"Guilty." Luca shot her an apologetic grin. "You're all making me—the clinic—look really good."

"Ciao, Pia!"

Luca turned in the direction Giuliana was waving—something she hadn't been able to do when she'd arrived here—the smile dropping from his lips again when he saw Fran corralling his niece and her dogs into the large courtyard. Giuliana called out a greeting again, and Pia quickly changed course toward them.

Fran's eyes caught his but she didn't cross over. Not that he blamed her.

"Scusi, Dr. Montovano, Pia is going to show me some things with the dogs."

"No problem." Luca grinned—not that Giuliana was hanging around to see if he wanted her to stay.

"Dr. Montovano?" His administrative assistant appeared by his side with a note in her hand.

"Si, Rosa?"

"We've got a patient who would like to be transferred here. His parents, actually. They say their son has lost hope."

"We don't have room," he said by rote, giving his head a shake, though his mind was already spinning with ways to make it possible. It wasn't the money—though that would help. It was the hope part. When a patient had lost hope...

"They're asking for intensive. Maybe a month."

We may not have a month.

"Perhaps if he came for a day. A chance to see the other patients so he doesn't feel so alone," Rosa persisted.

"What's his case history?"

He shouldn't ask. Knowing more about the patient would make him want to help.

A shard of frustration tugged his brows together. His gut was telling him to say yes. The staff had already made it clear they would be fine working with more patients. It was simply a question of finding the room. He and Pia could move out of *their* house, but after so much disruption he hated to move her again.

Out of the corner of his eye he could see Fran approaching the pergola as the girls and the dogs disappeared, leaving gales of laughter in their wake. Fran's cottage was wheelchair friendly. Close enough to the clinic's hub to access all the facilities easily.

"It's just the three of them, you say?"

"Three of who?" Fran asked.

"A new patient and his parents," Rosa jumped in.

"No. *Not* a new patient. I'm afraid it won't work," Luca interjected. "There's nowhere for him to stay."

"How about my cottage?"

Fran looked between the two of them, as if they were both ridiculous for not thinking of it in the first place.

"You would give up your cottage?" Rosa's eyes lit with relief.

"Of course I would. Anything! I'd leave right now if that helped."

"And abandon Pia?" Luca shook his head. "Leave her with the job half-done—not to mention the other patients you've taken on—before your contract is up?"

Fran's eyes shot to his, striking him like a viper. Neither of them was talking about Pia and he knew it.

"I'm hardly *abandoning* anything. I only have a few days left anyway."

Of course she would leave. What had he thought would happen after last night? Had he really thought ripping his heart open and letting his whole sorry story pour out would keep her here? *No.* Quite the opposite. He hadn't thought at all. He most likely repulsed her now.

"I would *never* let my patients down," Fran shot back before he could get a word in. "I'm talking about the cottage. I can stay anywhere. The patients can't."

He waited for her to state the obvious. That he needed the money. He needed *her.*

"Rosa." He forced himself to speak calmly. "Would you please give us a moment to discuss Miss Martinelli's housing arrangements?"

"Of course, Dr. Montovano."

If he wasn't mistaken, Rosa gave the tiniest hint of a smile before she reluctantly headed back to the office. Italians loved a passionate fight, and from the speed of the blood coursing through his veins this was set to be explosive.

"So, what's your big plan? To camp out on one of the sun loungers? Or are you going to whip one of the cottages into shape with one of your feel-good projects?"

Luca knew he was being unreasonable. Knew there was bite in his bark.

"I'll stay in town. Commute in like the other doctors. Besides, with my father coming—"

"What?"

"My father. You know he's coming."

Luca shook his head. He remembered her mentioning something about a visit, but it hadn't really registered.

He couldn't believe Fran would humiliate him like this. Show a half-finished clinic to a man renowned for his exacting attention to detail. A man who with a few swift strokes of his keyboard could save the clinic from oblivion. Fran's father was the last person on earth he wanted crossing the entryway to Mont di Mare.

"Why would you do that? Why would you invite him here?"

Fran took a step away from Luca, as if the question had physically repelled her.

"He's my *father*. He wants to see the clinic. Meet the people I've been talking about all summer. You of all people should know how important family is."

Luca looked at her as if she'd slapped him. Her remorse was instant, but it was too late to make apologies. The warmth she had once seen in Luca's eyes turned into inaccessible black, his pupils meshing with his irises as if there would never be enough light for him to see any good in the world. Any hope.

His lip curled in disgust, as if by inviting her father here she had betrayed him. "What's the point in bringing him here if all you're going to do is leave? Showing Daddy what a good little girl he's raised?"

"You don't mean that."

"Oh, I do, *chiara*." He closed the gap between them with one long-legged stride. "Has this been *fun* for you? Playing at a mountainside clinic while the rest of us are struggling to survive?"

Fran opened her mouth to answer, then thought better of it. Her heart ached for Luca. Ached to tell him everything—but not in the state he was in now. Unbending. Proud. Hurt. There was hurt coursing around that bloodstream of his—she knew it—but it didn't change the facts. She loved him, but if inviting her father here meant losing Luca but saving the clinic, then so be it. Her father was coming whether Luca liked it or not.

"Tell the new patient to come." She forced her voice to sound steady.

"For how long, Francesca? Where's your crystal ball? A day? A week? How many days do you foresee here before I have to tell this miserable wheelchair-bound boy and everyone else here that they will all have to go?"

"Whatever you feel is best. Now, if you'll excuse me, I have a patient appointment to keep."

Fran forced herself to turn away and walk calmly toward the clinic, trying her very best not to let Luca see that her knees were about to give way beneath her.

She knew anger and fear were fueling Luca's hateful comments. Of *course* she wanted the clinic to flourish. She wanted everything in the world for him. She wanted *him*!

Couldn't he see it in her eyes? In her heart?

Leaving wasn't the plan. *Staying* was the plan. The dream.

But her father was a facts man. He needed to see things for himself. Touch the stone. Scour the books. Observe the work. He'd never invest in a dream he didn't think could become a reality. And for the first time since she'd rung her father and asked him to jump on a plane as soon as possible, she felt a tremor of fear begin to shake inside her, forcing her to ask herself the same question again and again.

What have I done?

CHAPTER SIXTEEN

LUCA RUBBED THE kink out of his neck. A night in his office hadn't achieved anything other than darkening his already-foul mood.

"They're just about to land, Dr. Montovano," a nurse called out to him.

He pushed up and away from his desk and strode toward the helicopter-landing site.

Against his better judgment, he had approved the new patient's arrival.

It was Francesca's doing. Of course.

Not literally, but he'd heard her voice in his head each and every time he'd tried to say no. If he was going to go down, he might as well go down in flames.

He looked up to the sky to see if he could catch a glimpse of the chopper. They usually headed in from Florence, but this sound came from the east. Nearer to the seaside airport.

Unusual.

It was all unusual. This hospital transfer was happening much earlier than normal.

He huffed out a laugh. As the patient's stay would no doubt be short, they could at least eke a few more sessions out of his early arrival.

See? He shot a glance toward the bright sky. *I'm still capable of seeing the silver lining.*

The whirring blades of the helicopter strobed against the rays of sun hitting his face. He closed his eyes against the glare, taking a precious moment to relish the fact that the clinic was still here to help. Might still make a difference.

A day? A week? He didn't know how long he'd have with this boy, but he would do everything in his power to show him that giving up without a fight was sounding a death knell. And dying young…? That wasn't going to happen on *his* watch.

By the time the chopper landed, he had realigned his features into those of a benign clinician. Just as well. The first face he saw was his patient's.

A scowling teenage boy who looked intent on proving that nothing and no one would improve his lot in life.

Luca stepped toward the helicopter with a grim smile.

Giancarlo Salvi. Seventeen years old. An able-bodied teen turned quadriplegic after a late-night joyride went horrifically wrong.

He took another step forward and saw the boy's scowl deepen. And why wouldn't it? Luca was able-bodied. Strong. Vital. *He* had the ability to walk toward things— and away from them.

The moment froze in Luca's mind—crystalizing as if it were a beacon of truth.

No matter how powerless he felt, he still had choices.

Energy shot into his limbs, and without further ado he helped the crew unstrap Giancarlo's wheelchair.

Destiny wasn't just something you haphazardly fell into.

Destiny was something you shaped.

* * *

Fran tucked herself behind a thick cascade of greenery near the pergola when she heard voices. The last thing she wanted to do was distract Luca during this crucial time. Or drag out the duffel bag she'd hastily jammed her things into before cleaning her cottage to gleaming perfection before the new family arrived.

She needed to get it to the car so she could meet her father at the nearby airport. He'd called a few minutes ago and asked for a ride. Something about the helicopter he'd chartered being delayed. The excuse sounded sketchy, but maybe it was his way of having some alone time before he saw the clinic.

A nervous shudder went through her. Once she'd brought her father here, Luca might well decide he never wanted to speak to her again. But if that was the cost of keeping the clinic alive, she could just about live with herself.

Fran let the stone wall behind her take her weight for a moment as she fought the sting of tears. When she'd invited her father here, to see if he thought the clinic was worth investing in, she'd thought she was doing the right thing. Now she was riddled with doubt.

Her father liked cars, not people. His passion wasn't health care. Or dogs. The only reason he'd said he would invest in Canny Canines was to finally bring his daughter home.

She swiped at her eyes when she heard voices on the other side of the wall. The last thing she needed was to have a member of the staff—or worse, Luca—find her blubbering away.

She tuned in to the female voices. A pair of nurses whispering something about the newly arrived patient insisting the helicopter must stay until he had deemed the place "worthy."

Fran's blood boiled on Luca's behalf. The place was *exemplary*!

Her jaw set tight as she tugged Edison in closer to her and listened more closely when the voices changed.

"This is where most of our patients like to spend their downtime."

Fran peered out from behind the froth of summer blossoms at the sound of Luca's voice. He was just a few meters away, guiding a teenage boy and his parents through the archway and out to the walled garden with the pool. This area always won people's hearts. An infinity pool on the side of a mountain overlooking the sea... What wasn't to love?

"You've got to be kidding me." Disdain dripped from the teenage boy's every word. "Your paralyzed patients hang out by the *pool*? Why? So they can see what everyone else gets to do for fun?"

Luca eyed the boy silently for a while. He didn't need to check Giancarlo's charts to know fear of failure was behind the boy's words. It was obvious that whatever treatment he'd been receiving had been palliative at best.

"Didn't your previous physio involve any pool time?" Luca asked finally. The bulk of his patients had done at least a trial run in a pool, if not an entire program of hydrotherapy.

"*Si,* Dr. Montovano." The boy's voice still dripped with disdain. "They just threw us quadriplegics in the pool and whoever bobbed up first won a prize."

"Giancarlo! *Amore*, he's trying to help." His mother admonished her son in a hushed tone, but her flush of embarrassment betrayed the frustration she was obviously feeling.

Despite himself, Luca felt for her. A parent trying to do her best in an already bad situation. His thoughts shot to Fran. She'd been doing the same thing. Taking a bad situation and doing her very best to make it better.

Why hadn't he given her a chance to explain?

"Not all patients are necessarily up to pool work. Isn't that right, Dr. Montovano? My son's concerns *are* valid."

Luca nodded in Giancarlo's father's direction and gave his chin a thoughtful stroke, trying his best to look neutral as he processed the parents' different approaches to their boy's disability.

The father was accepting his son's bitterness. Failure. As if it were a done deal.

The mother? He could see her love knew no boundaries. That she was willing to give anything a shot if it meant bringing back her little boy.

"Not all facilities are equipped to deal with patients in hydrotherapy scenarios. We're one of the lucky ones."

"Lucky enough to be on a mountaintop and hide all of us cripples away, you mean."

Luca stared into Giancarlo's eyes, not liking what he saw. The bitterness. Rage. The loss of hope. All reflected back at him as if they were mirrors into his own soul.

A movement caught his attention. Edison. The Labrador was running into the garden, chasing after a tennis ball.

"You let *dogs* roam around here?" Giancarlo still sounded irritable, but the tiniest bit of light in his voice and the flash of interest in his otherwise-dull eyes told Luca all he needed to know. He still had hope. Despite everything, the boy still had hope.

Luca looked up and saw Fran slowly walking toward

them, her hand making a sharp signal to Edison that he should sit in front of Giancarlo's chair.

The parents were looking between Luca and Fran for answers. Was this her way of asking him not to give up hope?

"*Buongiorno.* I seem to have lost track of my assistance dog." Fran unleashed her warm smile, instantly relaxing Giancarlo's parents.

The Fran Effect.

"*Per favore.* Allow me to introduce Francesca Martinelli—"

"Like the cars?" Giancarlo interrupted, the first hint of a smile discernible on his face.

"Exactly like the cars." Fran nodded. Then smiled.

Better than sunshine.

The next twenty minutes or so passed in a blur as Edison became the center of attention.

Giancarlo's parents watched, wide-eyed, as Fran and the assistance dog exhibited a wide array of skills. Holding the boy upright if necessary. Retrieving objects and placing them in Giancarlo's hands. Manipulating his electric wheelchair around hard-to-negotiate corners. Going for help if necessary. She was bringing smiles to the lips of three people who Luca was certain hadn't known much, if any, happiness in the months since their lives had been changed forever.

By the time Fran had finished with her display, the Salvis—including Giancarlo—were committed to staying.

"Let me organize one of the other doctors to show you around." Luca heard the note of caution in his own voice. Fran had performed a miracle and still he wasn't happy. What was wrong with him?

Once Dr. Murro had been found and was showing the Salvis around the facilities, Luca wheeled on Fran.

"What the *hell* do you think you're doing?"

Bewilderment swept across Fran's features. "What do you mean? I was helping! Didn't you want them to stay?"

"Not this way. Not when I don't know how long I can offer them treatment. Don't you see what you've done?"

"Offered him hope? Offered him a new way of looking at the world?" Defiance rang in her every word.

"Stop!" He spoke too harshly, too cruelly for someone who felt as if his heart was breaking.

Fatigue hit him like a ton of bricks. This couldn't go on. He only had so much energy, and what little of it was left would have to go to Pia and the clinic.

"Will you please just stop?"

Francesca looked at him, her eyes held wide as if a blink would shatter her into a million pieces.

In them—in those crystal-clear blue eyes of hers— he saw myriad messages. Confusion. Tenderness. Pain.

She turned away without a word, and as she disappeared around the corner he knew in the very core of his being what the universe had been screaming at him all these weeks—he was in love with Fran.

"Dr. Montovano?"

A knock sounded at Luca's office door. Enzo Fratelli, one of the physios, cracked the door open a bit wider, obviously hoping for an invitation to come in.

"Si?" Luca flipped over the pile of paperwork he'd been working on. No point in Enzo seeing all the red ink. Not before he'd found a way to tell the staff.

"We all want you to know we appreciate how much work you've been putting into getting the clinic up and running."

Luca pushed back from the desk, suddenly too tired to pretend any longer. "Is it worth it, Enzo? Really?"

He gestured for his colleague to sit down. He knew he'd given up a lot to come and work here—a life in Florence, assured work at a busy hospital.

"*Si, Dottore.* Of course it is." Enzo sat down, concern pressing his brows together. "What makes you doubt it?"

Money. Debt. The idea of doing this whole damn thing without Francesca to remind him of the bright side.

"What if I've been wrong?"

"About what?"

"The location. About having the clinic here at Mont di Mare."

"But that's half the draw. Surely you of all people would see that?"

Luca nodded, looking away from the appeal in the young man's eyes.

"I'm not saying the idea of the clinic needs to come to an end. Perhaps we'd be better off relocating to a city. Florence. Or Rome, maybe."

"I don't understand." Enzo shook his head. "This is your family's land, no? Your heritage." He opened his arms wide. "Being up here at Mont di Mare, breathing the mountain air, seeing the sea, being part of the sky, the meadows—all of it—is every bit as healing as the work I do in the physio rooms."

He tipped his head to the side, as if trying to get a new perspective on Luca. See him afresh.

"You've been working too hard, Dr. Montovano. Surely now that Francesca's father is here you can relax a little. Go enjoy a prosecco on the terrace—"

Everything inside him grew rigid. He'd not yet given himself a chance to process his feelings about Fran—about loving her—and now her father was here.

It didn't matter now whether or not *he* wanted her to stay. With her father here to influence—to persuade, see things through a cooler lens—everything would change.

"Where are they?" Luca strode out from behind his desk.

Enzo put up his hands and took a couple of steps back. "*Scusi, per favore, Dottore.* I thought you knew. She's showing him around the clinic now. Lovely time of day— seeing the sunset from up here."

Luca didn't hear what else Enzo was saying. He was running down the corridor, his blood racing so hot and fast he was surprised he could still see. It didn't matter. Blind. Breathless. However he found her, all he knew was one thing. He had to find Fran.

"Did you notice this, Papa? The date carved into the beam?"

Francesca watched as her father lifted his fingers and touched the date almost reverently.

"It's very beautiful, Francesca. How old did you say the village was?"

"It's medieval."

Francesca whirled around and all but collided with Luca. Her heart rate shot into hyperdrive and the power of speech simply left her. She'd been hoping Luca would stay holed up in the main clinic building, like he usually did, while she gave her father the grand tour. If her pitch was successful she could at least leave with a clean conscience, if not an unbroken heart.

"*Scusi?*" Fran's father turned, too. "You are?"

"Papa," Fran interjected, "this is Luca Montovano. Remember I told you about him? The clinic director. Luca, this is my father, Vincente Martinelli."

The men introduced themselves with a sharp handshake and the type of solid eye contact that seemed more gladiatorial than friendly.

"It's a delight to have you here, Mr. Martinelli," Luca said solidly, his eyes not affording her even the most cursory of glances. "I suppose Francesca has told you what a mark she has made here?"

Fran felt heat creep into her cheeks as the two most important men in her life turned toward her. She didn't like being the center of attention at the best of times, and it was all she could do to keep her feet from whipping around and pulling her away toward the wildflower meadows she'd grown to love so much. Wildflowers she'd never see again if her father took the bait.

"Of course." Her father gave Luca a discerning look. "Francesca has spent most of my time here so far singing your praises."

"Papa!" Fran protested. Feebly.

She knew as well as he did that she'd been completely transparent. Glowing like a love-struck teen despite every effort to present the clinic as an outstanding business opportunity.

"I was simply…simply making the point that the entire vision here at Mont di Mare is Luca's. From the cobblestones to the first-class clinic. None of this would exist without his insight. His…um…"

Stop talking, Fran.

No, don't!

This is your last chance.

And so she plowed on. Detailing the clinic's mission. The work they'd done so far. The work she would have loved to do if she could stay, but she knew with Luca's talent he'd surely find more therapists. The best, of course. Only the best.

Despite the charge of adrenaline coursing through

her, Fran saw that Luca's eyes softened as she spoke. The gentle light that warmed the espresso darkness of his irises got brighter and brighter as she carried on. Her eyes dipped to his mouth. Those beautiful lips she would never be able to kiss again.

Forcing herself to meet Luca's gaze, Fran charged ahead with her final appeal. If her father saw what she did in Luca he would do the right thing and accept her offer to leave today in exchange for starting a charitable foundation to support the clinic.

"Like yours, Papa, Luca's drive is pretty much un-paralleled. In such a short time he has…he has… He's…"

Completely stolen my heart.

Luca's eyes widened slightly, his right eyebrow mak-ing that delightful little questioning arc she'd grown to enjoy watching out for whenever his curiosity was piqued.

"I've never seen anyone render my daughter speech-less, Dr. Montovano. You seem to have made quite an impact."

"She's made a similar impression," Luca replied, his eyes never leaving hers as he spoke.

"Francesca is very loyal. Always has been," her father replied with a decisive nod.

And then Luca saw it.

The switch.

One moment Francesca was looking into his eyes as if her life depended upon it, and the next…

There wasn't a soul in the world except for her fa-ther. The very light in Francesca's eyes changed when her gaze shifted to her father. A steely determination re-placed the gentle glow.

Thank goodness he hadn't dropped to his knees. Begged her to marry him as he wanted to.

We could do it. Together we could do anything we put our hearts and minds to.

This was his fault. He'd cut too deep to hold on to her affections. Been too harsh. She was a gentle soul who needed to be cared for as generously as she was generous in giving her heart to others. Again, he'd taken a bad situation and made it worse. *So* much worse.

The clinic had been meant to redeem him, not ruin him.

Luca's lungs strained against the pain. As if his heart was being ripped from his chest.

"Per favore," he finally managed. "Do continue with your tour. I wouldn't want you to miss anything before you both return to the States."

"Return?" Vincente turned to his daughter. "Haven't you spoken with him?"

Fran opened her mouth to try to explain but, much to her horror, her father beat her to it.

This wasn't the way it was meant to happen. She was supposed to be on a plane, heading far, far away from the man who had stolen her heart, before he knew she'd made one last-ditch effort to help.

"Si, Dottore," her father began. "My daughter, as you have obviously come to discover, is fueled by grand thoughts and ideas. She called me with a simple proposal."

"Which is…?"

Fran shivered to hear the chill in Luca's voice. She hadn't done it to hurt him. Far from it. She'd done it for *love*! Emotion choked the words in her throat and all she could do was watch, wide-eyed, as her father continued.

"Francesca said your clinic could do with a large financial injection. A way to get more rooms prepared for patients and increase cash flow. One of the ideas she suggested was to run her own business from here."

"Is this true?"

Luca turned to her, forcing her to meet his gaze.

Fran nodded, wishing the mountain would swallow her up and leave her in darkness. She was no business mogul. It was just an idea.

"It won't work. A single investment," her father continued, seemingly oblivious to the heartbreak happening right in front of him.

"Papa—no!"

"Hear me out, Frannie, I didn't get where I am today by being sentimental."

Fran's eyes darted toward Luca. He'd drawn himself to his full height, dark eyes flashing with emotion. He gave a curt nod. He'd hear her father out, but she knew any love he might have had for her was gone.

"Martinelli Motors isn't all about cars. Did you know this, Dr. Montovano?"

"I'm afraid I didn't. Fran hasn't told me much about you at all."

A hint of coldness shivered down Fran's spine. How could she? She barely knew her father.

"How would you feel about Francesca managing a charitable trust on behalf of Martinelli Motors here at the clinic? As well as her assistance-dog business."

"Papa?" A flutter of hope lit up Francesca's eyes while Luca remained stoically silent.

"Fran's been talking about starting a trust for ages, and I have to say I didn't put much stock in it. But now that I've seen the clinic, the passion with which my daughter approaches the business—"

"This is *not* her business," Luca interrupted.

"No, not now—but if I were to put money into it then she would, of course, become a partner."

"I think there's been a misunderstanding," Luca said, his eyes once again glued to Fran. "There is no part of this business that is for sale."

A pin might have dropped in a city two hundred miles away and Fran would have heard it in the silence that followed.

"Are you crazy?" Fran finally regained the power of speech, her eyes appealing to Luca to use common sense. *She* was the emotional one. Not him.

His refusal to answer made her even angrier. Now he was just being plain old stubborn.

"Papa. *Don't* let him refuse your offer. The clinic needs the trust. I will do anything to make that happen."

Much to her astonishment, her father raised his hand in protest. "I think Luca knows his own mind well enough. I'm not going to force the money down the poor man's throat."

Luca gave him a curt nod of thanks, then turned to walk away.

"Luca, please—wait!"

"I think I've heard enough." He began to stride toward the far end of the village.

"Luca, please," Fran pleaded once they were out of earshot of her father. "None of that went the way it was meant to."

He turned on her, chest heaving with exertion. Fran pulled herself up short, teetering on her tiptoes, reaching out toward him to try to gain her balance.

And that was when it dawned on him.

A truth so vivid it near enough brought him to his knees. He'd been fighting the wrong battle. Fighting a truth that had raged like a tempest within him from the day he'd laid eyes on her.

Love was about faith. Deep-seated belief. And trust.

Fran would never ask her father—a man with whom she was only just beginning to have a proper relationship—to pour money into something, *someone*, she didn't believe in. She saw something in *him*. Trusted *him*.

And here she was, after all the horrible things he had said to her, reaching out with nothing but love in her eyes.

He held out his hands to her and pulled her to him. With every fiber of his being he loved her.

He cupped her face with his hands and tipped his forehead to hers. "Francesca, I've been a fool. You aren't trying to take anything from me, are you?"

"Of course not," she whispered. "I love you."

"How?" His hands dropped to her shoulders and he held her out so she could take a good look at him. "*How* can you love me when I have been so horrible?"

A gentle smile played upon her lips before she answered. "Everything you do is motivated by love."

"And how do you come to that conclusion, my little ray of sunshine?"

"Because a lesser man would have given up long ago," she said, giving a decisive nod. Her voice grew clearer, stronger, as she continued. "A lesser man would've stayed in Rome. Put his niece in a home. Hidden from everything he was ashamed of. Instead you confront the things you hate most about yourself on a daily basis."

"I owe it to Pia—"

"You didn't owe her an entire *clinic*!" Fran said, the light and humor he so loved finally returning to her eyes.

"But her mother, her grandparents—it was *my* fault they were all in that car."

"It wasn't your fault the truck lost control. You didn't

make it cross the median strip. You didn't ask it to crash into you! I know it was awful, but it was *not* your fault."

Luca pulled her close to him, feeling her heart thud against his chest. He drew his fingers through her hair and asked aloud the question he'd wondered again and again.

"How can I deserve you?"

Fran pulled back, eyelids dropped to half-mast, and quirked an eyebrow. "You don't—yet."

"I beg to differ, *amore*, but you are standing in my arms."

"That doesn't mean we've made any decisions yet, does it?"

"About what?"

"About my business. Canny Canines. If you think I'm going to give it up just because you've won my heart you've got another think coming."

"Does this mean I'm going to have to go groveling to your father?"

Fran crinkled her nose. "I thought you didn't want his money?"

"I don't," Luca admitted. "But I *do* want something far more precious to him than any amount of money he has."

A twinkle lit up Francesca's eye. "Oh, yes? And what could *that* possibly be?"

"I think you know exactly what I'm talking about, Francesca Martinelli." He pulled back from her, folding her small hands between his as he knelt on the ground in front of her. "I would very much like it if you would consider becoming Francesca Montovano."

Fran's eyes filled with tears as she nodded. "Yes. Yes, please. I'd love to."

Luca rose to his feet, picked Francesca up and twirled her around, whooping to the heavens all the while.

When he put her down he tipped his head toward her and murmured, "As you're going to be staying awhile, I suppose it would be a good idea for you to agree with your father about the whole Martinelli Trust thing."

Fran's tooth captured her lower lip and he felt her fingers pressing into his hands.

"Do you mean it?"

"I can hardly refuse the opportunity to help needy children, can I?"

"Luca Montovano…" Fran sighed as she rose on tiptoe to give him the softest kiss he'd ever known, "I'm going to love you until the end of time."

He cinched his arms around her waist, pulling her in for a kiss so rich with meaning there was no mistaking how long he would love her in return.

"Forever and ever, *amore*. Until the end of time."

Two years later

"Dante!" Fran clicked her fingers, a proud smile lighting up her face as the dog padded off to the opposite side of the patio and returned with her padded shoulder bag.

"Is he getting so heavy that you can't get out of your chair?" Luca laughed, taking the diaper bag from their latest canine family member and handing it to his wife with a tender smile.

Fran gazed down into the eyes of her son—a teeny-tiny replica of his father.

"Pia's been bringing him to the gym. Getting the other patients to use him as a weight!"

She laughed at the memory of one of the poor girls straining to lift him to shoulder height, Pia leaning forward, her hands ready if he dropped more than a millimeter.

"I think he gains a kilo every other day!" She tickled the tiny tip of his nose. "Besides, why would I want to move when I have everything I need right here?"

"And what's that?" Luca asked, settling into the patio chair alongside Francesca.

"You know exactly what I mean, but as you've asked, I will tell you." Fran held up a hand and ticked off her list on her fingers. "A gorgeous man, a big furry dog, the most handsome son a woman could ask for and, of course, the view."

She reached out her hand, closing her eyes tight as the tickle of sparks that still tingled and delighted her each and every time she and Luca touched took effect.

"The view *is* rather spectacular," Luca said.

When she opened her eyes she saw he wasn't facing the mountains, nor the broad, lush valleys below them, not even the sea sparkling in the early morning sun. Luca—her husband, her love—was looking directly into her eyes.

* * * * *

*If you enjoyed this story, check out
these other great reads from
Annie O'Neil*

HEALING THE SHEIKH'S HEART
HER HOT HIGHLAND DOC
SANTIAGO'S CONVENIENT FIANCÉE
THE NIGHTSHIFT BEFORE CHRISTMAS

All available now!

MILLS & BOON®
Hardback – August 2017

ROMANCE

An Heir Made in the Marriage Bed	Anne Mather
The Prince's Stolen Virgin	Maisey Yates
Protecting His Defiant Innocent	Michelle Smart
Pregnant at Acosta's Demand	Maya Blake
The Secret He Must Claim	Chantelle Shaw
Carrying the Spaniard's Child	Jennie Lucas
A Ring for the Greek's Baby	Melanie Milburne
Bought for the Billionaire's Revenge	Clare Connelly
The Runaway Bride and the Billionaire	Kate Hardy
The Boss's Fake Fiancée	Susan Meier
The Millionaire's Redemption	Therese Beharrie
Captivated by the Enigmatic Tycoon	Bella Bucannon
Tempted by the Bridesmaid	Annie O'Neil
Claiming His Pregnant Princess	Annie O'Neil
A Miracle for the Baby Doctor	Meredith Webber
Stolen Kisses with Her Boss	Susan Carlisle
Encounter with a Commanding Officer	Charlotte Hawkes
Rebel Doc on Her Doorstep	Lucy Ryder
The CEO's Nanny Affair	Joss Wood
Tempted by the Wrong Twin	Rachel Bailey

0717 GEN STD HB

MILLS & BOON®
Large Print – August 2017

ROMANCE

The Italian's One-Night Baby	Lynne Graham
The Desert King's Captive Bride	Annie West
Once a Moretti Wife	Michelle Smart
The Boss's Nine-Month Negotiation	Maya Blake
The Secret Heir of Alazar	Kate Hewitt
Crowned for the Drakon Legacy	Tara Pammi
His Mistress with Two Secrets	Dani Collins
Stranded with the Secret Billionaire	Marion Lennox
Reunited by a Baby Bombshell	Barbara Hannay
The Spanish Tycoon's Takeover	Michelle Douglas
Miss Prim and the Maverick Millionaire	Nina Singh

HISTORICAL

Claiming His Desert Princess	Marguerite Kaye
Bound by Their Secret Passion	Diane Gaston
The Wallflower Duchess	Liz Tyner
Captive of the Viking	Juliet Landon
The Spaniard's Innocent Maiden	Greta Gilbert

MEDICAL

Their Meant-to-Be Baby	Caroline Anderson
A Mummy for His Baby	Molly Evans
Rafael's One Night Bombshell	Tina Beckett
Dante's Shock Proposal	Amalie Berlin
A Forever Family for the Army Doc	Meredith Webber
The Nurse and the Single Dad	Dianne Drake

MILLS & BOON®
Hardback – September 2017

ROMANCE

The Tycoon's Outrageous Proposal	Miranda Lee
Cipriani's Innocent Captive	Cathy Williams
Claiming His One-Night Baby	Michelle Smart
At the Ruthless Billionaire's Command	Carole Mortimer
Engaged for Her Enemy's Heir	Kate Hewitt
His Drakon Runaway Bride	Tara Pammi
The Throne He Must Take	Chantelle Shaw
The Italian's Virgin Acquisition	Michelle Conder
A Proposal from the Crown Prince	Jessica Gilmore
Sarah and the Secret Sheikh	Michelle Douglas
Conveniently Engaged to the Boss	Ellie Darkins
Her New York Billionaire	Andrea Bolter
The Doctor's Forbidden Temptation	Tina Beckett
From Passion to Pregnancy	Tina Beckett
The Midwife's Longed-For Baby	Caroline Anderson
One Night That Changed Her Life	Emily Forbes
The Prince's Cinderella Bride	Amalie Berlin
Bride for the Single Dad	Jennifer Taylor
A Family for the Billionaire	Dani Wade
Taking Home the Tycoon	Catherine Mann

MILLS & BOON®
Large Print – September 2017

ROMANCE

The Sheikh's Bought Wife	Sharon Kendrick
The Innocent's Shameful Secret	Sara Craven
The Magnate's Tempestuous Marriage	Miranda Lee
The Forced Bride of Alazar	Kate Hewitt
Bound by the Sultan's Baby	Carol Marinelli
Blackmailed Down the Aisle	Louise Fuller
Di Marcello's Secret Son	Rachael Thomas
Conveniently Wed to the Greek	Kandy Shepherd
His Shy Cinderella	Kate Hardy
Falling for the Rebel Princess	Ellie Darkins
Claimed by the Wealthy Magnate	Nina Milne

HISTORICAL

The Secret Marriage Pact	Georgie Lee
A Warriner to Protect Her	Virginia Heath
Claiming His Defiant Miss	Bronwyn Scott
Rumours at Court (Rumors at Court)	Blythe Gifford
The Duke's Unexpected Bride	Lara Temple

MEDICAL

Their Secret Royal Baby	Carol Marinelli
Her Hot Highland Doc	Annie O'Neil
His Pregnant Royal Bride	Amy Ruttan
Baby Surprise for the Doctor Prince	Robin Gianna
Resisting Her Army Doc Rival	Sue MacKay
A Month to Marry the Midwife	Fiona McArthur

MILLS & BOON®

Why shop at millsandboon.co.uk?

Each year, thousands of romance readers find their
perfect read at millsandboon.co.uk. That's because
we're passionate about bringing you the very best
romantic fiction. Here are some of the advantages
of shopping at www.millsandboon.co.uk:

* **Get new books first**—you'll be able to buy your
  favourite books one month before they hit
  the shops

* **Get exclusive discounts**—you'll also be able to buy
  our specially created monthly collections, with up
  to 50% off the RRP

* **Find your favourite authors**—latest news,
  interviews and new releases for all your favourite
  authors and series on our website, plus ideas for
  what to try next

* **Join in**—once you've bought your favourite books,
  don't forget to register with us to rate, review and
  join in the discussions

Visit **www.millsandboon.co.uk**
for all this and more today!